A Compendium of Short Stories

Leslie James

Pen Press

© Leslie James 2013

All rights reserved

No part of this publication may be reproduced, stored in a retrieval system, or transmitted in any form or by any means, without the prior permission in writing of the publisher, nor be otherwise circulated in any form of binding or cover other than that in which it is published and without a similar condition including this condition being imposed on the subsequent purchaser.

First published in Great Britain by Pen Press

All paper used in the printing of this book has been made from wood grown in managed, sustainable forests.

ISBN: 978-1-78003-546-8

Printed and bound in the UK
Pen Press is an imprint of
Indepenpress Publishing Limited
25 Eastern Place
Brighton
BN2 1GJ

A catalogue record of this book is available from the British Library

Cover design by Jacqueline Abromeit

To Dot.

For all the patience and all the help you have given me.
My love and thanks to a true friend. But most of all, for being a truly great wife.

A Brief Biography of the Author

Born Ronald Leslie James Chilvers in the year of the Lord 1927 on 21st July within the sound of Bow Bells, London, England.

Lived in Surrey until voluntary joining the regular army in 1945, completing my training at the 28th Training Battalion in Belfast, Northern Ireland. Served in Europe, Italy, Egypt and Saudi Arabia with the East Surrey Regiment, the Military Police and the Royal Sussex Regiment.

Now living in Peacehaven, East Sussex and a member of The Royal Society of St George (Sussex Branch).

Book One

Land Army

I'm the only son of Florence and Leslie McDonald, this being due to complications at my birth, which took place on 21st July 1923. I was born Leslie James McDonald at my parents' farm not far from Hickstead in Sussex. Now Mum was of a very slight build, only 5ft 4ins tall, but with a very womanly figure. Her hair was red and her eyes a pale green. A real lady, always ready to do anyone a good turn. She originally came from Henfield in Sussex. Now Dad was 6ft tall, built like a Highland bull, with ginger hair, blue eyes and a deep gravel voice. He liked to have a pint or two after work of his homemade cider, and he was from Bannockburn, just south of Stirling in Scotland.

Now Mum and Dad ran the farm with two farmhands and a herdsman and later on, when I wasn't at college studying, I enjoyed working for Dad as I got to drive the tractor. All that fresh air and the hard work did me the world of good because when I was 16 years and six months old, I stood 6ft 2ins tall with a body that anyone of my age would be pleased with. When out shopping with Mum in Brighton or Eastbourne, some of the remarks from the females were: "Hi, big boy" and "Just ask and I'm yours". Mum used to smile and say, "Don't let them worry you, son. Just remember you'll have no worries in the future."

The Second World War was still going on but Dad being a farmer had been exempt. But not his two farmhands. No matter how hard he tried to get them exemption, they still had to go. When I was 16 and six months, I decided to leave college and work full time with Dad. I found the work very hard going, sometimes working up to 20 hours a day and I was always ready for my bed. It was the long hours that led to Dad having the accident with the combined harvester.

He was taken to The Royal Sussex Hospital in Brighton and remained there for four weeks. In that time he lost three toes from his right foot. That's when Mum said, "That's it, we must contact the Ministry and get help."

Mum did just that and within the week we had two fine, buxom Land Army girls arrive, Jill and Jenny, and the promise of more in a short time. Two more of them arrived by the Ministry's own transport; they had come from Scotland and were two very big, strong, strapping and good-looking girls, who had requested a change from being "lumber Jill's" in the forests of the North. Their names were Jane and Flo, who straight away got on well with Jill and Jenny and all four of them told Mum and Dad no to be worrying and got on with the job. They seemed to have the herd working for them as soon as they took over the milking from Dad and the maintenance of the sheds. Even the milk yield went up; it must have been the woman's touch.

Once the girls had things running to their liking, you could see the relief in Mum's and Dad's faces. Dad still managed to do the ploughing with the tractor in the two lower 40-acre fields and even took over the chickens and egg marketing from Mum.

Every now and then, Dad and I went to the Friday stock market in Hailsham to catch up with the local farmers' gossip and to see if we could better our own stock. I left

Dad to do that job while I went to the post office to collect the local papers for Mum. It was then that Mrs Printer the postmistress, or if you like, May, said, "Hello, my lovely Boy. When are you going to marry one of my lovely daughters?"

I must have gone very red because everyone in the shop started to look my way and had a giggle. They also had great big grins on their faces. One of them even said, "I've got just the right daughter for you and I wouldn't mind having you as a son-in-law."

May must have been about 40 years old and was a big woman with light, mousy hair, blue eyes and a very good sense of business. Her husband, Fred, was of a similar build and the same age; a much regarded member of the local community. They had this small-holding just outside of the village had been supplying most of the local tradesmen with soft fruits and root crops and making a good living out of it.

On one of the market days, as usual May and Fred had a stall showing and selling their produce when a commotion erupted. Fred went to have a look. One of the show bulls had been frightened and had somehow got out of its pen. Fred, being the man he was, took up the pole to hook it into the ring on the bull's nose. The bull somehow managed to avoid his attempt and swung round, hitting Fred with its rear end. Fred was sent flying and with some considerable force hit the upright of a pen and fell into a lifeless heap. When the ambulance arrived the crew did not say anything but looked very worried. On arrival at the hospital, Fred was pronounced DOA, dead on arrival. Two days later their only son, also called Fred, managed to find some alcohol, took the family truck, lost control on a bend, hit a tree he too was pronounced DOA.

The whole village, man, woman and child, turned out and joined May and her two remaining daughters for the double funeral.

Not long after that, with a brave attempt to carry on, May had told some of the village folk that the small-holding held too many memories and had decided to sell up. She did just that and bought the village post office and general store.

It was now just over a year later and this was then May, in that loud bellowing voice, told me about the girls waiting at the station.

"Did you know that you have four more of them lovely Land Army girls waiting for you at the station, Leslie?"

"Thanks, May. I best be off and see about collecting them."

I found Dad, who was having some good old friendly banter and conversation with four of his old farmer friends. I told him the good news and only after he had finished his pint of cider did he say, with a good old belly laugh, "We had better be off to the station before these four rogues get their hands on them we don't want that to happen, do we?"

With hand shaking all around and a lot more friendly banter, we left them and headed for the station.

As we arrived, one of the girls called, "Taxi!" and then they all laughed.

I apologised for the transport.

"Don't worry, big boy, we shall have to get used to this."

And with that, two of them got up front with Dad and I joined the other two in the back. We pulled into the yard and Mum was standing there with the other four girls, Jane, Flo, Jenny and Jill.

"My goodness, what am I going to do with all of you?"

It was then that I thought of the old farm workers' cottages.

"Mum!" I called out. "Why not open up the two farm cottages?"

"That's a jolly good idea, son."

So now we have four to each cottage, which they all said was very nice and it was not that long before we spotted smoke drifting from the chimneys. The girls had certainly arrived.

Time passed and one evening, when I was 17 and five months old and while Mum, Dad and I were having our evening meal, I asked them if I could join the army.

Mum said, "We have been expecting this," and they both said that they would sooner I ran the farm.

It was Dad who said, "I think you have already made your mind up."

I said I would very much like to Go and they both said so be it.

Two weeks later I went to the recruiting office in Lewes where the recruiting officer, an old army sergeant major, said that with my education he would put me forward for officer training. It was three weeks later that the letter arrived. I had to report to the barracks at Colchester in Essex for 12 weeks' primary training before going on to Sandhurst for officer training.

Right from the start I knew I was going to enjoy the army. My 12 weeks' training at Colchester went very quickly and I then found myself with two other candidates on our way to The Royal Military Academy at Sandhurst in Surrey. On the train I had time to think about what lay ahead as things were happening very quickly and it was just a little concerning.

The training at Sandhurst was very hard but extremely professional. It took just over a year and I managed to hold my end up and passed with good results. We had the usual passing-out parade, which Mum and Dad attended. I was now just over 19, with a two-week leave pass safely in my pocket. Second Lieutenant McDonald took his parents home to the farm.

Back on the farm, the girls had everything working in tip-top condition and Mum and Dad were looking to be in good health so I had no need to worry about them.

Ten days into my leave I received a letter to say that my request to join the Gurkha Regiment had been granted and I was to report to Shornclife Training camp in Kent to meet serving officers, who would arrange my travel papers and documentation so I could join the first battalion in Hong Kong. I was also given another 21 days' embarkation leave, which pleased Mum.

The girl's had a surprise for me. I was outside the next morning with a big smile and a pitch fork, waiting for orders from them the mucking out that had to be done. I was really enjoying myself back on the farm as I could see that Mum and Dad were that much happier and Dad had now got used to his slight limp and the girls thought the world of them both. But all things must come to an end when you are happy with a situation, only mine came a bit sooner than I expected.

It was about halfway through my leave and I was sitting outside the chicken house after a hard day's work having a glass of cider with Mum, Dad and the girls, when the army dispatch rider arrived.

He looked over at Dad and said, "Lieutenant McDonald?"

Dad pointed me out and the young lad walked over, saluted and said, "Would you please sign my book, sir, and I'm told to tell you this dispatch is to be opened right away."

I replied, "Thank you. Would you care for a glass of cider before your return?"

"That's very kind of you, sir," he said. "I sure would. I've not had any cider for a very long time."

With that the girls took over and it must have been about an hour later that he finally left the farm a very happy young man with more than one colour of lipstick on his face.

In the meantime, I had taken my orders to my bedroom. My embarkation leave had been terminated and as from then I was to report at once to the commanding officer of The Royal Engineers at Bovington in Wiltshire. My joining the Gurkhas had also been cancelled but my promotion had been confirmed, so with joy of my promotion and a feeling of sadness on my not going to the Gurkhas, I told my folks and the girls and started to pack. I was ready to go but decided to take one more day, on which I arranged to take Mum and Dad to a show at The Royal Theatre in Brighton with dinner after. On the way back, Mum had a little cry and Dad sat very quiet.

The next morning the taxi arrived at ten o'clock the driver loaded my bags and I said my goodbyes and then I was on my way, but even so, I had a lump in my throat.

The journey to Wiltshire was uneventful and I was met at the station by a very smart driver and a spotless car, which told me that I was going to a very well organised unit. On arrival, the duty sergeant, who was immaculately turned out, informed me that I was to report to the commanding officer at 1700 hrs in number one dress here at the orderly room and a Private McGregory had been assigned as my batman. He had already taken my luggage and was waiting and watching just out of earshot to show me my quarters.

I returned the sergeant's salute, turned and said, "Okay, McGregory, let's see what awaits me."

I was very pleasantly surprised; my quarters had everything I needed. Looking over at McGregor I said, "Okay, what do I call you out of earshot of anyone, McGregory?"

"Well, sir, I'll answer to Mac."

"Okay then, it's Mac. So let's unpack and see what my number ones looks like, shall we?"

"If you would like, sir, I'll unpack and see to your number ones. You may like to take this opportunity to take a shower, sir."

"Now that's a very good idea. Well thought of, Mac."

I had my shower, shaved and Mac had made a good job of my number one uniform and he had added the extra pip on my epaulets so I made my way to the orderly room where the orderly sergeant was waiting for me.

He saluted, saying, "Would you please wait why I tell the CO you're here, sir?" and with that he disappeared.

It was only then that I realised I knew nothing of the CO I was about to meet. My thinking was cut short by the return of the sergeant saying, "This way if you please, sir."

I walked into the office, saluted and said, "Reporting as requested, sir."

I could see he was a big man even if he remained seated because he filled the chair he was seated in. He had bright blue eyes a good head of red hair neatly cut army style and a very rosy complexion. He was also giving me a good looking over and then realised his manners and stood up, offering me his hand and saying, "I do beg your pardon but you are just what I was hoping for. Please sit yourself down."

An orderly appeared with a tray of tea and a good selection of biscuits. Once he had departed, my new CO started by saying, "My name is Angus McMorris, Lieutenant Colonel Angus McMorris and I'm from Laurencekirk on the east coast of Scotland, just north of Montrose, and I'm old enough to be you're father. Right, now that I have got that off my chest, I'll tell you what you are here for. First of all, this a training unit and your job will be the supervision of the instructors and then training the personnel into their special units so I have set out a plan for you to start with which you can change as and when you think fit to do so. We shall be getting a lot more troops in within the next three weeks so we are going to be very busy and going to need a lot more huts erected to accommodate them. I suggest you start with that. You're in the deep end, my friend, so get McGregor to show you the camp and one more thing, you are now second-in-command as from now so it's over to you, Lieutenant."

I left the office in a complete daze went back to my quarters and called for Mac.

"I'm going to need help, Mac. Who is the most experienced man in the unit who has some knowledge of the workings of an army engineering unit?" He said he knew of two of the older men. I replied, "Go and bring them back here at the double. At the same time go to the MT office and get me a jeep. I hope you can drive, Mac. At the double, Mac, at the double.

With a "Yes, sir" he disappeared.

The two men arrived. They must have been running as they both stood there panting and blowing like two overweight old-age pensioners, but found the strength to mumble and with a very poor salute, say, "We were told you wanted to see us, sir!"

"Come in and find yourselves a chair or something to sit on."

Mac then arrived, saying, "Sorry, sir, they will not give me a jeep."

"Okay. Give these chaps and yourself some tea, but before you do that, get the person you spoke to at the MT office on the phone."

There was a slight pause and then Mac said, "Sir. Sergeant Woods of the MT for you."

"Sergeant Woods, stop your blasphemy and just listen to me. I'm the second-in-command of this unit and when I send my batman to you with a request, you will comply. Now, you will personally bring a jeep to my quarters in five minutes or I'll have you placed in the guardhouse awaiting a court marshal. Do I make myself clear?"

With the three of them listening to every word I said, the whole unit would know that I'll stand for no nonsense but at the same time I felt guilty for using such a low trick, but I found out later that it had worked and the jeep arrived on time, so now I was the one you didn't want to mess with, so Mac told me.

"Mac, clear the mess off this table and let's get down to work." I looked over at the two men and said, "Well, you know who I am, tell me who you are."

They both stood up, the older-looking one started by saying, "Corporal Bull, five years' service with the Royal Engineers, sir."

"Corporal Sykes, five years also, sir. We joined up together, sir."

"Well, Corporal Bull, you sit this end of the table and you, Corporal Sykes, sit the other end. I want you to draw me a plan of the camp using the edge of the paper as the border. You have five minutes," and with that I left them to it.

I called Mac, saying, "Come on, let's have a look at the jeep." It was not very clean and the tyres had seen better days. "Okay, Mac, take it back and tell Sergeant Woods I want it cleaned with a new set of tyres and it's to have a full service. And I want to see it with its service record and log book outside my quarters at nine o'clock tomorrow morning." Mac was about to drive off when I said, "And take that silly grin of your face," because I knew why he was grinning.

I returned to find both corporals had completed their drawings.

"That's fine. The only thing that I notice is that one of you has made the NAAFI a lot bigger than the other."

Mac returned and said everything was okay.

"Now, Mac, go and tell the orderly sergeant I want to see him right away."

The phone rang and Mac said, "The CO wants to see you, sir, when it's convenient!"

"That means right away. You three stay put," and off I went to the orderly room.

When I got there, the CO was waiting for me.

"Come in and sit down," he said. Once again I got that looking over, but he was smiling and said, "I hear and have seen that the camp is a lot more alive now. Well, just thought I would like to say you have my full backing so go and get on with it, you're doing a great job and thank you."

I stopped at the MT Office, called for Sergeant Woods and told him I wanted transport with a driver to convey myself and three others around the camp in 30 minutes outside my quarters. I got a "Yes, sir" with a smart salute.

I walked back, and on my arrival I said, "You three have 20 minutes to go to the NAAFI and get some refreshments." It also gave me time to think.

The transport arrived. I got in and said, "The NAAFI" and with an old-fashioned look from the driver we proceeded and stopped outside.

I said, "Go and get Bull, Sykes and Mc Gregory out here at the double."

All three came running, still chewing a bun of some kind, and piled into the back of the 1,500-weight truck. I told the driver to go to the open ground at the far end of the camp and on our arrival I went to the back of the vehicle.

"Right, Corporals Bull and Sykes, come with me. Driver, take Mac back to my quarters and then come back here."

I started to walk and said, "We are going to put 24 billets here that will hold 20 personnel in each and four more as washhouses on this site. Now it's up to you to help me do it so start thinking.

"That's an easy one, sir," said Sykes. "All we need is the equipment."

"That's very good Sykes. Sit over there and make me a list."

He did just that in the meantime, myself and Bull had paced out the area and found out that we could put more than the 24 I had first thought of. So it was, then, with the list of materials that Sykes had made out, the transport arrived and I said, "Orderly room please, driver," and as soon as we arrived, "You all wait here while I see the CO."

"Come In, Leslie. Twice in one day, well, I hope it's good news," he said.

"I think you will find it so, sir. This is a list of what will be required for 30-plus timber-framed billets. I'll be pegging out the ground tomorrow for the bases and once we have the equipment I say six to eight weeks and we should be up and running. Just one other thing I would like you to do and that's to sanction the promotion to sergeant of the two men I have outside."

"Okay, let's have a look at them. Bring them in."

I told the orderly to bring Bull and Sykes in. The colonel, with the same stern look, looked them over, asked them about their service with the unit and gave me a nod. Then speaking to them, he said, "You had better read part-one orders at the request of the second-in-command. I'm making you both up to sergeants as from now."

They both said, "Thank you, sir," saluted and left the office.

After some more pep talk, I to left the office to find the two newly appointed sergeants waiting to thank me.

I said, "I think you are going to earn your promotion, so be at my quarters at 0800 hrs properly dressed, and muster as many hands as you can find. That goes for you as well, driver, 0800 hrs with your vehicle outside my quarters."

It was at that point that the orderly sergeant appeared.

"You wanted to see me, sir?" I had completely forgotten I had asked to see him.

"Yes, that's right, sergeant. A bit late now, but that's my fault. Now let me see, today is Friday and I want a full turnout on Monday at 0730 hrs outside the orderly room of everyone, and I mean everyone. On no account is there to be anyone excused this parade, except the colonel and yourself. You will be at the main gate stopping anyone going out or coming in. Now, you see I mean everyone will be on that parade and they are to be in working dress. Get this on part-one orders tonight. There are to be no exceptions."

Monday and Mac had me up and dressed ready for the parade and disappeared to be on the parade himself. I walked out right on the dot of 0730 a Sergeant Godfrey, who I had not seen before, called everyone to attention, walked over and saluted in a very smart manner, saying, "The unit on parade, sir."

"Thank you, sergeant. Stand the men easy and have the cooks assemble on the right and the MT section on the left with the person in charge of that particular section with them.

"Yes, sir. But begging your pardon, sir, the colonel has just arrived and is coming this way."

I turned, saw where he was standing, marched over to him and saluted, saying, "Good morning, sir."

He had that big smile and said, "Would you mind if I join you? I've always wanted to do this but could never find the time or an excuse to do so. What's yours?"

"Like you, sir, I just wanted to see what I'm going to have to work with."

"In the next ten weeks we are going to be very, very busy and I thought this was the best way to do just that and that they will get to know me."

"You don't have to worry about that because I'm told you have already made your mark, But come on, let's see what we have. Let's look them over. What are those two groups out front for?"

"They, sir, are the cooks and the transport section. They are the reason for some of the discontent and bad behaviour we have in camp at the moment. I would very much like your permission to make changes in both sections."

"You have it. As I have already told you, you're second-in-command and the running of this camp is your problem. I'm afraid that for the moment with my being tied up at GHQ, I'm going to have to leave it entirely up you so if you have changes to make, then make them."

"Thank you, sir."

We both looked the men over with the CO asking the NCOs what kind of training they did daily. "Not a lot, sir" was what most replied. "We have no equipment to do any training."

I turned to Sergeant Godfrey, saying, "Make a note and see me after the parade."

It was now the turn of the cooks. The cook sergeant shuffled forward, gave a very bad imitation of a salute and said, "Cooks on parade, sir."

The CO went completely white, looked around at me and then back at the sergeant, saying, "You are a complete and utter disgrace. You're dirty and smelly. Lieutenant, have this man taken to the guardroom. I want him put on orders."

He took one look at the rest of the cooks, saying, "As for you lot, you have 15 minutes to get clean up and get back on parade. Sergeant, see these men off the parade ground."

It was the MT's turn. He took one look at them, saying, "Sergeant Woods, be at my office 15 minutes after this parade," and with that he just walked away, saying to me as he passed, "You have your work cut out."

It was seven months later when I joined the CO outside the orderly room to see the first two fully trained units leave for destinations unknown to us. The CO acknowledged their departure by saluting each leading truck. On the departure of the last truck, the CO said, "Come into my office the three of you," and as we passed the orderly sergeant he called out, "Let's have some tea in here."

The tea arrived and the sergeant left the room.

"Be seated, gentlemen. Now, let's get down to business! You two sergeants had better read part-one orders because as from this moment you are both promoted to sergeant major. And as for you, Leslie, I've informed HQ of the very hard work you have had to put into the building of this camp and requested that an early appointment to captain be made."

At that point, a knock came on the door and the orderly sergeant walked over the CO and said, "You did say you wanted to see the reply to your signal to HQ rights away, sir!"

"Yes, thank you."

The door closed and the CO look at the signal, stood up, walked over to me and said, "Let me be the first to say congratulations, Captain, your appointment has been confirmed. And that's not all today. I also have something to celebrate. Due to your efforts I've also been promoted to full colonel."

All three of us saluted and shook his hand, saying how pleased we were for him. He called for the sergeant to break out the drinks. "And stay and have one yourself. Gentlemen, I say thank you all for your efforts. One last thing, gentlemen, in the next three days I would like you to arrange for someone to take over from you. That will bring us to Friday from which date you are all granted 14 days' leave and four days after your return we are going to get a new intake of 300 men and 40 ATS cooks and administration staff, along with 20 new officers and 30 senior NCOs and sergeant majors. We shall need another 40 plots laid out for more huts, so you are going to have your work cut out. The huts will be here when you get back from leave so before you go, see that whoever you put in charge understands the situation and you will want to see the bases laid ready and maybe some of the huts erected on your return. May you all have a very good leave, gentlemen."

My leave went very well. The farm was running well and Dad had managed to acquire more land adjoining the lower section. That meant we now had over 4,000 acres and a flourishing egg contract with two of the larger stores. Mum still kept busy looking after the girls, who in return, took great care of her and Dad and I'm pleased to say, on the other hand, Dad has got himself doing some of the paperwork with the aid of Mary, and Mary also kept me informed of the goings on and about Mum and Dad's health.

As leave goes, this one went very quickly and I found once again myself having to say goodbye to a crying Mum, who had made sure that I had plenty of fried chicken and eggs to take back with me. I shared this with Mac, who had returned the day before, and then took a walk around the site, bumping into the two new sergeant majors, Bull and Sykes.

We were very pleased with what we saw. All the bases had been laid and three of the huts had been completed.

I reported to the Colonel first thing the next morning.

"Glad to have you back, Leslie," he said. "Got some news for you! Sit down, laddy. As from now I'm posted to GHQ permanently and you are now in full charge of this training establishment and the higher establishment want to increase the turnout by 100% in the next six months and the size of the camp will be increased by 100 acres to accommodate the personnel and equipment that will be arriving in the next two weeks. Some of the equipment will be here tomorrow. I have to ask you if you are prepared to take over, as if not, a suitable officer will be appointed. I've already told them at GHQ you are the one for the job, so how about it, my boy, what do you say? You'll more than likely get a promotion out of it."

"I must say, sir, you are putting a lot of trust in me, but yes, sir, I would like to prove that your trust in me will prove to be right, and thank you, sir, thank you."

Leslie it has been a great pleasure working with you and I'll be leaving tonight as I must report to GHQ first thing tomorrow morning. So once again, I have to drop you in at the deep end. If at any time I can be of help to you, you know where to find me."

It has been 18 months since I took over the camp and our training programs have been a great success and the camp has a very good reputation and I was very pleased with myself. That was when I got a call from GHQ – the colonel wanted to see me! I was also told to bring my batman and uniforms as I would be attending a working dinner with the general and he likes to dress for dinner. It would be a long weekend. What did the general want me for? What was in store for me was anyone's guess!

As it turned out, the colonel had dropped me in it once more but this time it worked out to my benefit. The general said that my name had been put forward by the colonel due to the fact that I had run my present camp and attained first class results and would I like to take on the job of starting a new camp in Devon?

"I see you have had a recent promotion to captain but I'm sure I can arrange it that you would start off as a major if you take on this very important task."

"That's very kind of you, sir, and I would like the job. May I ask if I'd be permitted to take some of the personnel with me?"

"I'll agree to that," the General said and with that we continued with our dinner.

The new camp was at Dunkery Beacon south of Ilfracombe in Devon, situated on both sides of the river Exe, on which we kept the men extremely busy training by building bridges and then taking them down again. The camp was a great success; not only did we keep up with our own training program, we had units posted to us from the Canadian and American Engineers, as they say, "Learning to do it the Limy way". The camp was a beehive but a very good beehive with me as queen bee.

Mac had collected my mail, in which there was a letter from Mary informing me that Mum was not very well and she had called the doctor in to see her. I told Mac to pack a bag, informed GHQ of my intention, arranged with the second-in-command to keep me informed and gave Mac my home number.

On arrival at the farm, I could see that Mum was not just unwell, she was very ill and arranged for her to be seen at the local hospital. The news was not good. Mum had a terminal illness and was told to have plenty of rest. I had a word with Mary, who was going to get a nurse in to look after Mum. I think the news hit Dad very hard and Mary had one of the girls take over the paperwork and at the same time keep an eye on him. I found it very hard to leave but I could not stay any longer and returned to camp.

The following Wednesday I had a phone call from the colonel with an invitation to a party. I called Mac and told him to pack our bags and arrange for the car to be available for him to drive. I made my way to the bank in Dunkery Beacon to arrange for me to be able to cash a cheque now and then. The bank manager was an elderly chap and said that the arrangements would be made and after looking at my account told me that it was a very healthy one for someone so young. He carried on by saying that I had six £600,000 and would I like to invest some of it? I'd never realised I had that much in the bank. I replied that I would see him on my return and have a talk about investments.

It was a long drive so we took turns at the wheel but eventfully arrived to a very warm greeting and was able to shower and change.

Mac asked if it would be all right if he popped home to see his folks as they only lived 20 miles away, so I told him to take the car and to have a couple of days to himself but to be back in time to for the return to camp.

The next morning the colonel and I went to his golf club, had a few drinks and a walk around the course, which is when he told me what he had been up to at GHQ and that as from yesterday, he was now brigadier and would be needing an officer of my rank to be his assistant at GHQ.

"If you would like the job, it's yours, and you can bring Mac with you if you take the position. Let me have your decision in two days."

That evening there must have been about 25 guests at the party, to which I was introduced to everyone. One particular, very beautiful, young lady about the same age as myself whom I could not take my eyes off and also just happened to be the newly appointed brigadier's niece and was seated next to me, much to my pleasure. It was as if we had come out of the same pea pod; we got on right from the start and before long I realised that I had told her everything about myself and all I knew was that her name was

Annabella, which, with a big smile, she said she would in my case answer to Ann.

It was then that the brigadier come over and said, "I hope you two are behaving yourselves."

Me, I just went completely red and Ann just laughed and said, "Now, Uncle Richard, I'll tell everyone what you get up to if you don't leave us alone," and with that he made a hasty retreat.

We made arrangements to meet the next day at a very pleasant restaurant. We had a great meal and a very nice musical show. In the evening, I was about to ask about the next day when Ann said, "I understand that you may be joining my uncle at his place of work."

It was then that I realised the weekend had ended. How the time goes when you are having a good time.

"Would you mind if I kept in touch?" I asked. Her reply was what I was hoping for and she put arms around me and kissed me, saying she looked forward to our next rendezvous.

The next morning Mac arrived promptly at eight o'clock. The brigadier, who had opened the door, said, "You had better come and have some breakfast, Mac. You don't mind if I call you Mac, Mac?"

"That's very kind of you, sir."

It was about 8.30 when the doorbell rang. It was Ann saying, "I've just come to see Leslie off, Uncle."

"You had better take him into the lounge, then. But before you do that, say hello to Mac, he's Leslie's batman. They shook hands and then we retreated to the lounge.

It was very pleasant saying goodbye again. She said, "Let's keep in touch, Leslie. I've got a funny feeling about our meeting." I replied that would be my wish and my pleasure to do, so we kissed with a bit more passion this time and I was over the moon.

The brigadier opened the door, saying, "Come on, you two. One of you has a lot of thinking to do." So that's how my weekend ended.

On the way home I asked Mac how he felt about going to GHQ to work.

"Blimey, guv, that's among the big boys."

"It would mean you would have to be a sergeant and probably have to drive as well as doing the batman bit."

He did not reply right away, but eventually said, "If you go, sir so shall I." So it was agreed, we would accept the brigadier's offer.

The next morning I phoned him with my decision. He was more than pleased and said, "Thank you, my boy. I shall need you to report here at GHQ in four weeks, that should give you time to sort yourself out down there."

I said, "Thank you, sir. See you in four weeks." I called for Mac. "Go and get Bull and Sykes to report to my office on the double, and don't mention anything about the move."

Just like old times, puffing and blowing and red in the face, both were standing at the attention in front of my desk. I looked them over and thought how lucky I had been in having these two to help me through the setting up and with the training programmes over the last few years.

It was Sykes who said, "Anything the matter, sir?"

"I've had my eye on you two and I think that you both need some exercise so I've arranged for both of you to attend a school where I'm sure they will see to it that you will have plenty to do and you must certainly loose some weight. You are to report to the officer's academy at Sandhurst in Surrey on the 1st of next month." With that I just burst out laughing saying, "You should have seen your faces!"

I called Mac, who had been standing outside the door and said to him, "You can take that grin off your face. Go away and come back properly dressed, sergeant!"

Now that we were all in the one room, I told the two sergeant majors of my intended move and that on their appointments they would probably have to go their separate ways.

"But in any case, I'll see that you have my location and if you need my help just ring and don't forget to keep in touch."

The next day a Major McComas arrived. A tall, dark man who had obviously been Wounded, he said, "The brigadier sent me along to help out with your move."
"You're just the chap I'm looking for," I said. "Mac, get the jeep and show the major the camp, every last bit of it, and anywhere he wants to go, and then come back here.

So the brigadier is helping out by sending me my replacement, I thought.

It must have been just over the hour later when Mac and the major returned.

"Okay, Major, let's go for a drive."
I might just as well get this over with, I thought, so I drove down to the village, went into The Red Lion pub and said, "The lunch is on me. By the way, I'm Major Leslie McDonald, OC of this training establishment. You have joined with the brigadier's blessing, so how do you feel like becoming the new CO? Because that's what you will be as from ten days from now. Don't worry, I'll see that you have the top NCOs working with you and all the help I can give you."

We had a very good dinner with couple of pints of cider, which got me thinking of home, Mum and Dad. So the last thing I did as CO was to give the two sergeant majors, Mac and myself 14 days' leave. I also phoned Ann, asking her if she would like to come to the farm and meet my parents. She said she would be pleased to do so and would meet me at the farm. I then phoned Mary and asked how things were with Mum.

The news was not good and Dad was very quiet and did a lot of walking around the farm, but Mary always had one of girls go with him.

It was Ann who arrived at the farm first and Mary took her to the house to meet Mum and Dad. My late arrival was due to prolonged goodbyes at the camp and road hold-ups on route. When I arrived, Mum and Ann were like old friends and Dad had one big smile, pulled me to one side and said, "You have a good one there, my boy."

That night I took Mum, Dad, Mary and as many of the girls that could get away, along with the girl of my dreams – Ann – to the pub and a good time was had by all.

The next day, being market day, Ann, Dad and I went to the market just to keep up with local gossip. We left Dad with some of the other farmers and I took Ann to the post office. As soon as I walked in May, shouted across the shop in that deep loud voice, "I've got a bone to pick with you, my lovely boy!" And as usual the whole shop looked towards us and I felt Ann take a firmer grip on my arm.

"No need to worry, my love, her bark is just a way to let me know she's seen me and she's trying to make me go red, like the old days."

May then come round the counter put her arms around me and gave one great big kiss full on the lips. When she put me down she called her girls and said, "Come and say hello to Leslie."

They were more discreet and gave me a peck on the cheek. In the meantime, May had put her arm around Ann and was leading her off towards the back of the shop. Looking over at me, she said, "Don't just stand their, help my girls and serve some of my customers."

It turned out to be a bit of fun, until I had to use the till. The two girls soon showed me and then the two smiling women appeared and seemed to be the best of pals. That was when May started to get complaints from her customers. They were saying, "Why couldn't lovely boy serve us?"

Ann and I looked at each other, waved and made a hasty retreat back to find Dad, who was sitting on his own looking down at his pint of cider.

"Okay, Dad, time to go back home."

He downed the rest of his drink, mumbling, "It's not liked the old days, Leslie my boy! Not like the old days."

Mary was waiting for us, saying Mum had taken to her bed and the nurse had sent for the doctor. We went to see her but she was sleeping so we left and waited to see what the doctor had to say. His stay was a short one, just saying see that she gets plenty of rest.

The next day she was a lot better and even insisted on a walk around the farm and talking to all the girls and getting all there names right. Dad was making a fuss of her until she told him to stop fussing and to go and get her a glass of cider.

Mum peacefully passed away that night, leaving us all very bereft. It was the first time I had seen Ann and Dad cry and I walked out into the farmyard, meeting all the girls crying as well. I could not hold it in any longer and just joined them all. I phoned GHQ and had words with the brigadier, who said, "Have another ten days' leave. But I do need you here, things are getting a bit warm under the collar.

The next morning I had Mary and all the girls in for a talk regarding the running of the farm and told them what I thought. I then said, "Please let me have your feelings."

They all agreed that Mary should take charge, but they could do with some more help. I phoned right away, while they were all there, to the contact the farm had with the ministry and they agreed that more help would be sent as soon as possible. That seemed to please everyone.

In all, six more arrived in the next five days. I told Dad what would be taking place and maybe he would be around to give advice as needed. This pleased him and he said he was pleased with the arrangements. Ann, who had stayed with me, came to the bank with me the next morning and asked to see the manager to make arrangements for Mary to be able to make withdraws to save Dad any problems. It was then that he explained that some six months earlier, Dad had signed the farm over to me with a very large sum of money, so if I would do the signing he would do everything he could to help Mary in the future.

"I also see that your account with this bank now stands at £1,300,000," he added.

I was flabbergasted at the amount. We, Ann and I, walked in silence for a long time. I stopped, faced her and said, "Would you marry me, dear Ann?"

"I would be very pleased to marry you, my dear Leslie, but I think you had better ask my dear uncle as well as me."

Ann left for her home and I had a final meeting with Dad, Mary and the girls, and then returned to GHQ to see what was making the brigadier's collar so warm and to ask him about marrying Ann.

When he did arrive, he was in a bad mood and everyone just got out of his way so I made sure he spent some time on his own until he had cooled down.

He poked his head out his office door and said, "Please come in, Leslie." He told me the reason for his outburst. Apparently he had been denied a posting to Europe as he was wanted at GHQ. "So if I'm not going, nor are you. Now tell me about your latest problem. I told him that everything had gone off very well and that Ann had been a real brick and helped me no end and would he mind if I married his niece. He gave me one of those long looks he's so good at and then the smile.

"Good god, man, I've been waiting for you to ask me. I'll be glad to get her off my back. She's been a real worry for me and I'll be very pleased to give her away. Have you any dates in mind? Only I'm going to have another go at getting an overseas posting and it may mean you having to come with me. Would that be all right with you?"

"Well, I've been home posting just like you so a spot of seeing the world would be okay with me. I'll have to ask Ann, but I'm sure it will be all right. You do need someone to look after you, sir!"

"Come on, Leslie, let's go to the mess and have a drink or two. Tonight the drinks are on you."

The end of the war in Europe had taken place, and the brigadier never did get his overseas posting, but I did. As it so happens, an engineer's officer was required to take a fully operational bridge building regiment to Europe to repair and build bridges.

The brigadier said, "Just up you street and it will mean your get another pip."

I was told by the area general, the Right Hon Sir James Barnet, that I must be operational in ten weeks. I explained that I was getting married in ten days and would it be okay if I had ten days' leave within the next ten weeks.

"It's all right with me, but you had better have a word with the brigadier and okay it with him."

"I think it will be all right, sir. You see, it's his niece I'll be marrying!"

He gave a big bellowing roar, saying, "If you're that good at organising, I'll have no worries about your ability to get the show on the road."

On my return from leave, Mrs Ann McDonald and I made our home at the farm. Awaiting me was a signal from GHQ confirming my promotion to Lt Colonel, along with orders to report asap. So that night, my new wife, Dad and all the men and girls at the farm, not forgetting Mary, celebrated at the local pub.

The next morning, after a tearful farewell, I managed to get to the waiting taxi.

On my return to GHQ I found Sergeant Mac waiting for me, saying, "I have all your gear packed and the car ready for you, sir."

The brigadier made it quite clear I was not wanted there and that I should have been on my way to Wiltshire, but before I left I made some enquiries regarding the location of Bull and Sykes and arranged for them to be assigned to my new unit.

Our trip to Wiltshire was uneventful, that is until we arrived at the camp itself. The gate was unmanned. I told Mac to stop the car and then lent over and sounded the car Horn.

A window slid back and an arm of an unknown person appeared and waved us in. I kept my hand on the horn, which made the arm wave a bit faster, and a sergeant opened the door with no hat on, tunic unbuttoned, smoking and holding a cup of tea with just a casual glance towards the car. He then waved us on as he was about to walk back into the guardroom. I got out of the car in a hurry banging my knee, which did not help matters.

I called out, "Sergeant! Stand still!" and walked over to the guardroom. "Sergeant McGregory, get everyone out and line them up."

I have never seen such a lot of dirty looking personnel as what came out. Sergeant McGregory walked over and saluted, saying, "I found these two were in the cells, sir."

"Take their names and have them report to you in 30 minutes in clean working Uniform. And they both stink so make sure they have a shower."

They both saluted, saying, "Thank you, sir"

"Sergeant McGregory, see that this lot don't move! No, on second thoughts, put them all in the cells."

There was a shout of protest from the sergeant but Mac was a big chap and the sergeant took one look and decided it would be better to cooperate and joined the rest, but still directing a lot of shouting and blasphemy towards us.

"Come, Mac, let's have a look around and see what we have let ourselves in for."

Our first building proved to be the orderly room with just one private drinking a cup of tea and who, on seeing a lieutenant colonel standing in the doorway, jumped to his feet spilling his tea. But he managed to stand to attention, spluttering out, "Good morning, sir."

"Good morning, Private. What's your name?"

"Private Clarke, sir."

"Well, Private Clarke, find the person in charge of this office and tell them to report to me here at the double and I mean at the double."

"Yes, sir," and with that he fled the office.

Even so it was nearly ten minutes before anyone appeared. The first was another private, who said his name was Private Williams and he was CO's batman. On being asked why he was here, he said he had been told by the CO to get him another bottle of gin and he was here looking for the officers' mess sergeant. That's when the orderly room sergeant major arrived in a state of undress. He was told he had five minutes to present himself properly dressed.

On his return, he was instructed to parade every last member of the establishment, officers, NCOs and men, on the parade ground in the next 20 minuets and to send Private Williams, the CO's batman, to me. That's when Mac and I went to CO's quarters and met Major William Murray, who was in a state of incoherent intoxication and was in no fit state to understand what was going on and could only mumble, "Where's that bloody Williams with my bottle of gin?"

"Mac, see that Williams gets the key to this door and tell him no one goes in or out. No matter what."

The parade ground was full and a very young first lieutenant reported, "Personnel on parade, sir."

"Why you, Lieutenant?" I enquired.

"I'm sorry, sir, but the second-in-command and the adjutant are both out of camp, sir. They did say they could be contacted if needed in The Star Hotel."

"Sergeant McGregory, get their details and request the MPs to arrest them and bring them back to camp."

"Yes, sir, right away. And the two prisoners have reported back, sir."

"That's good. Have one of them go to the cookhouse and get us something to eat and drink and tell them, whoever they are, that I want it brought here to the orderly room. And send the other one to me. We shall be in the CO's office."

Thank goodness, you smell a lot better. What's your name?"

"Black, sir. Private Black, sir."

"Right, Private Black. I'm going to need two men for batmen. Do you think you could be one of them?"

"Yes, sir. I would like that thank you, sir."

"How about your friend?"

"Knight, sir. Private Knight, sir. I feel he would like to be the other one, sir."

"Good, so be it, then. Have a look out of the window and tell me what you see."

"A lot of officers and sergeants, sir."

"Good. Go and call my sergeant in."

Mac knocked on the door saying, "The MPs have arrived, sir."

"Thank you, Sergeant."

The two officers, looking very bewildered, started to talk at the same time but I told them to shut up and listen. They stopped and I said, "I think you both better stop talking for as from now you are both under arrest and confined to your quarters pending court marshal. That will be all. Dismissed."

Outside was a very smart Military Police officer and a sergeant.

"Would you please come with me, out of ear shot of that lot?"

I explained to the officer who I was and that I had been sent by GHQ to take over this shambles and that I wanted complete security, no one in or out of the camp without authority from me or GHQ.

"And I mean no one, starting from now, and your men are to take over the guardroom as the first occupants are now in the cells, including the sergeant. And see that they all have a shower and an army haircut and plenty of drills until I can deal with them. Will that be okay, Lieutenant?

With a smart salute, a "Yes, sir" and a nod to his sergeant, off they went.

I called out, "I'll see you in the mess tonight, Lieutenant."

"Thank you, sir," he replied.

I walked back to the parade ground and said to the waiting officers and sergeants, "All ranks will be on parade tonight at 2000 hrs, formed up in companies on the parade ground. All officers will have with them full details of their company personnel. All ranks will be in working dress and no one will be exempt from this parade. Dismissed!

"Being a batman, Knight, you come with me. First, take me to the transport office."

I called for Mac. "Take Black with you and sort out our quarters and show him the ropes of being a batman."

"Yes, sir."

"It's this way, sir."

"Can you drive, Knight?"

"Yes, sir."

We arrived at a very old site hut but word must have reached them of what was going on because I got a very good salute from a short fat sergeant and I said I wanted a jeep outside my quarters at 0700 hrs in the morning, clean and with a full tank of petrol and its full service record and log book. And then in the next 24 hours, I shall need a full report of what transport you have and their condition and what you need to bring all transport up to first-class condition.

I could see him start to perspire at the thought of all the work he had to do.

"Come on, Knight, the plant yard, if you please.

As we walked through the transport yard, we disturbed a card school made up of sergeants.

I walked over and said, "You'll all be privates tomorrow if you don't get back to some kind of work," and walked on.

"Is it all like this, Knight? Don't answer that."

"Thank you, sir."

The plant yard was another shambles and the sergeant was even fatter. I told him the same, a full list of the condition and requirements in 24 hours.

"Right, Knight, show me my quarters, I've had it."

An MP walked over, saluted and said, "We have two officers in the guardroom, sir. A Mr Bull and Mr Sykes."

"Thank you. Have them shown to my quarters."

I told Mac, who said it would be nice to see them again.

They arrived under escort and all four of us had a good laugh with Black and Knight looking on. I called them over and said, "Take your pick of these very gallant officers."

It was Mac who saved the blushes.

"I've already allocated Knight to Mr Bull and Black to Mr Sykes, sir."

The next morning I informed Lieutenants Sykes and Bull of the programme being upgraded for the camp and they were to go out there and sort everyone out and bust some of them down in rank if necessary and promote those that looked like promising NCOs.

"But it has to be done in the next week because we need accommodation for 500 personnel in three weeks."

The MP sergeant asked to see me and said, "The guardhouse is full, sir. Can we release some of them?"

"Good idea, Sergeant. We need them working. But I'll see the sergeant on orders at 0900 hrs."

But that night the sergeant attacked the guard commander so badly that he was hospitalised. As for the sergeant, he was recaptured the same night by the MPs and in time he was given a three-year prison sentence.

My two trusty lieutenants had done a good job so I told them to lay off a bit but to make sure they were working. And work they did. We had all the huts up and in working order ready and waiting the arrival of our first draft of personnel one day early, so that night in the dining hall I saw that every man had a bottle of beer with his meal.

The following morning about 0830 hrs singing was heard coming from the road leading up to the camp; it was our new members marching from the station. They had full kit on and were lugging kit bags so I instructed Lieutenants Bull and Sykes to allocate them to billets as quickly as possible. First parade for them would be 0800 hrs Monday morning, outside the orderly room with all ranks in denims. That went for the two of them and myself.

Monday morning came and I walked to the centre of the parade, stood on a chair and said, "You had all better face me." I waited for things to settle down and then said, "You men are a special detachment sent here to be trained in road and bridge building in Europe. You have 12 weeks in which to accomplish this, so you will have to work very hard because for those that make it, there will be 14 days' leave and those that don't will join the new detachment and start again. You will now be formed into five groups, good luck."

In a very short time the camp was really humming and we had many visits from GHQ and others saying how things had changed and that the end product was always a first-class turnout. With the arrival of the ATS cooks and admin staff, things in all departments had made our camp into a happy one because the food was very good and the boy and girl relationship was an even better moral booster.

But now I was growing weary of my job and said to myself it's time to think of my family, so I had a talk with Ann, who agreed that a change would be a wonderful idea. I also had Mac promoted to regimental sergeant major so that he received a pension on retirement, which was due in about six months. So with this in mind, I asked Mac to accompany Ann and Dad by train to Stirling to survey the area for what would be our final home, telling him that if he would like, he could have the job of gamekeeper with a cottage for him and his family. He was over the moon. In the meantime I had made an appointment to see the brigadier, who just happened to be Ann's uncle, to start proceedings for my retirement in six months' time.

I'm now Lieutenant Colonel retired, along with my friend Mac, who also retired. We're on our way to my estate south west of Perth at a place called Kinkell Bridge, alongside the River Earn were Mac and I intend to spend some time with a rod and line.

Market Day Express

On The Buses Number One

After completing my training at Chiswick in South London to become a London Transport bus driver, I was reporting to Sutton bus garage in Surrey for an early start. But then I must expect that, being the new boy at the garage.

On reporting in, I was shown how to sign on and at the same time I was told they had nothing for me and I was to report to the garage in Clapham, South London. As soon as I arrived, they sent me out to learn one of their routes – the number 45. It's a very difficult route to learn in just one ride, so on my return I told the inspector that I was far from happy and would like to go out again, only to be told, "Sorry, mate, you're booked out on the next 45 due outside the garage in 20 minutes. You'll find your conductor in the canteen, his name is Achieves Smith-White."

Yes, you are right; he was one of our friends from Jamaica. He was a big one must have been 6ft 6ins tall and just as wide and he had a voice like a trumping elephant.

"Okay, man," he said. "We have some 15 minutes," so we sat at one of the canteen tables. That was when I asked him how he got such a posh name.

"Well, man, just call me Zac, everyone does. It's like this, man, I come from a very poor one-parent family and my mudeer was out looking to earn a shilling or two when she come across these two drunken sailors from the Royal Navy boat which was on a courtesy visit. Now they were both the worse for too much Jamaican rum but they struck up a bargain in which she agreed to accommodate them both in their needs. That was when they started to argue who was to be first and started to call each other by their names, such as 'Now you see here, Smithy' and 'No, you see here, Chalky'. Well, that's all my mudeer could remember nine months later when asked by the clerk the name of the father for the birth certificate, so they settled on Smith-White and in brackets Royal Navy."

Just as things were getting interesting, Zac said, "Okay, man, let's get going."

So we walked through the garage into the high street, only to find our bus waiting for us. It had arrived five minutes early as the crew had tickets for the Fulham football match and did not want to miss the kick off. I climbed up into the cab, adjusted the seat and waited for the first bell of the day.

Ding! Ding! I checked the mirrors, pressed the starter and we were off.

I was enjoying my first day of driving one very big red bus in South London. It was truly a great experience and one I shall always remember, especially today of all days. We were heading towards Stockwell when I suddenly realised I was not sure of the next part. I knew I had to take a left turn, but which one? I called Zac round, but all I got from him was, "It's no good you asking me, man, this is my first time on this route and I'm having a bad time of it back there."

"Okay, Zac, never mind. I'll take the next one," which I did. But as soon as I turned, I knew it was the wrong one because in front of me was a street full of traders and thousands of shoppers.

At first the traders were very helpful and moved their displays, that was until I reached the china stall. Now this trader, who's stall it was, proved to be a very unpleasant one and in "traders speak" and a bit of cockney rabbit, he told me very unpleasantly to reverse, as he was not moving for anyone. Me being the new boy on the block, I just did not know what to do, so I just sat there feeling very uncomfortable.

That was when the first missile arrived, hitting the windscreen plumb dead centre. It was an over-ripe tomato but before it had time to run down the window, it was joined by a barrage of every kind off rotten fruit and veg you could think off. It was very funny but at the same time, being my first time out, quite frightening. The passengers in the lower deck had done a runner, or like Zac, retreated to the upper deck. For me, I jammed the cab door firmly shut with my foot. It seemed like a very long time sitting there not knowing what to do, but a knocking on the cab door was a relief because I could see a bobby's helmet. Even so, I opened the door very gingerly, but the face had a great big smile on it.

"How did you get yourself into this mess?" he said.

My reply was, "All you have to do is take the wrong turn," and with that we both had a good laugh.

It was at this point that two London Transport inspectors arrived; one of them just so happened to be a gold badge and it could be seen that he was in a foul mood and he started by having a go at Zac.

I butted in by saying, "Hold on, mate, don't have a go at Him. It was me that took the wrong turning."

I thought he was going to have a heart attack because he went all red and his eyes were popping out so much that his glasses fell off his nose.

He said, "Don't call me mate. I happen to the area chief inspector."

I didn't like this so-called chief inspector so I just said, "So be it."

That's when the policeman said, "I think we had better think about getting this bus out of here," but it was too late, the second barrage of rotten fruit and veg started to rain down. The bobby and I made it into the cab but unfortunately the gold badge received a direct hit from a soggy wet lettuce on his left ear, knocking his hat all askew and his shirt front had the remains of a messy beetroot. I hoped he liked salad!

The bobby and I climbed out of the cab and I started to clean the screen. The bobby and the other inspector were talking to the traders. One of them was a lady trader.

"Come over 'ere, darling, let me give you a bunk-up. You have made my day."

Even the china chap came over, saying, "No hard feelings, mate."

Once more we were moving very slowly and arrived back on our route, but the inspector said, "You must take this bus back to the garage to be cleaned up. I'll be coming with you I wouldn't miss this for all the tea in china."

I drove into the garage to find the whole of the canteen staff, the maintenance staff and all the drivers and conductors waiting for us. The whistling and shouting nearly took the roof off and the crew and staff picked up Zac and carried him shoulder high towards the canteen.

I arrived back at Sutton garage to a grinning office staff, who all said in harmony, just like a lot of barbershop singers, "Report to Clapham garage tomorrow!" But that's another story…

Wedding Bells

On The Buses Number Two

As usual, I arrived early at the garage and signed on before making my way to the canteen to meet other crews, to listen to all the gossip and to find my brother, who is on the maintenance staff and still lives at home and so I get all the news of Mum and Dad. After coming out of the army, I found my own "pad" and didn't see them as often as I would have liked.

I still had plenty of time so I decided to walk up to the green where I took over from a driver on the 80A route. On the way, a bus on the 156 route passed me and standing on the platform was Fred, my mate and a conductor, who gives me a very rude gesture with his fingers. On meeting up, we both walk over to 'Arry, the inspector on duty, at the green, which is the terminus for ten routes.

Now 'Arry is a very good-looking chap and is well liked by all drivers, conductors and clippies. We find him talking to Madge the clippie, who is waiting for her driver.

We could not let this situation go without saying something and it was Fred who said very loudly, but looking at me, "Don't we take over from Tom? Looks like we shall have to tell him what's going on."

They both turned towards us, but before they could say anything Fred and I both bust out laughing and they joined in. It was at this point that our bus arrived and Madge's driver showed up.

Now the driver of our bus just happened to be Tom, Madge's fiancé and a very good friend of mine. When parking in line like this, the driver usually parks so that they can walk between the buses, but in this case you could not get a piece of paper between the two.

As Tom approached, I said, "I know you two are close but that close and I'm thinking it's time for you two to get married!"

After we'd all had a good laugh, 'Arry said, "Come on, you lot, get these buses moving."

That was when Tom said quite loudly, so that 'Arry could hear as well, "Don't like them brakes, Leslie. Take care," and with that I started my first journey of the day.

I did not think about what Tom had said about the brakes until we arrived at the stop outside the Odeon cinema at Rose Hill where I overshot the stopping point by about 3ft. From there on I gave a lot of attention to every stopping point because the brakes had not improved but had got worse and so on reaching the terminus at Tooting Broadway I went looking in the usual places for the duty inspector.

I eventually found him in a very dirty coffee shop, which did not please him because he had to leave his tea and toast. I explained to him about the brakes and that I was not happy and not prepared to go on with the bus. He just blew his top, calling me some very unpleasant and unprintable names in front of some intended passengers, of whom one lady made a formal complaint to the inspector asking for his name and mine. He then told me that I would have to take the bus back to the garage, so when I refused, he said, "Right then, I'll take it back and I'll have you suspended."

My conductor Fred and I climbed onboard and a very irate inspector climbed up into the cab and pressed the starter. It was when we got to Mitcham and he was having to go around the square that Fred said, "He's taking it a bit fast, Leslie."

And then it happened. You could see the tension on his face and he was standing on the brake but he was now experiencing what I had told him had been happening. With one almighty bang, he bounced off the high curb, hitting the car in front with such force that it sent it across the pavement missing a mum pushing a pram by a very small margin. The car finished up buried deep into the window of a very expensive antique showroom.

We helped the inspector out of the cab because he was shaking so badly and could not help himself. We sat him on the curb and Fred gave him a cup of tea from his flask. I walked over to the car sticking out of the shop window and saw that the driver and one shop man had been seen to. They did not look very good and the car driver was covered in blood.

The police arrived and we told them the story and they had a few words with the inspector and then said they would like him to accompany them to the police station. By then, other police had arrived and had everything under control and the sergeant and car left with one very shaken inspector.

After about 30 minutes, the garage breakdown vehicle arrived. Luckily, the crew chief was my brother, who was on the garage maintenance staff. I told him the same story we had told the police and Fred and I left the garage staff to get on with the recovery of the bus. We travelled on the next available bus back to the garage, where we both reported to the depot inspector, relaying the events, who after listening to our story said, "Check in with the running staff and carry on as instructed."

The next day, on signing on the worksheet, Fred and I were told to report once again to the deport inspector, who told us that both of us would be required to attend a general inquiry at head office at 55 Broadway at a later date.

It was five weeks later, with the garage chief inspector, our three union representatives, the two inspectors and my brother, Fred and Tom. We all travelled by Green Line coach up to London, without the Tooting Broadway inspector, who decided to make his own way.

Both Fred and I had made the effort to see that our uniforms had been pressed with buttons shining. It was the first time for both of us to see Number 55 Broadway, but not our last. On our arrival and after a short wait, we were asked to take a seat in front of the board of five men.

The chairman said, "Would you, Mr James, please tell us the story of the incident that occurred on Friday 13th May?"

I did just that, from the arrival of Tom and how close the bus had stopped to the parked one until we reported to the garage.

The chairmen looked towards Fred saying, "Have you anything to add?"

Fred's reply was, "I think the report you have just heard, sir, says it all and I have nothing to add."

We were asked to wait outside and after a short spell Fred and I were called in and asked to sign a typed statement. That was when I said that I would not do so until I'd had a chance to read it and that I would like to show it to my union representative before I signed anything. Fred backed me up, saying, "That goes for me too, sir."

You could see they did not like that so we scooped the papers up and Fred said, "If that's all, sir, we'll be on our way."

Once outside, Fred handed the papers to the chief inspector, saying, "We shall be making our own way back, sir."

The chairman just nodded and with that, Fred, Tom and myself made a bee-line for the city centre to do a bit of sightseeing.

Two weeks later and once again we were summoned to the chief inspector's office, only to be told that the enquiry was satisfactory and no one at Sutton had anything to worry about.

However, our next visit to 55 Broadway was not so pleasant as it was an inquiry into the Tooting Broadway inspector's behavior, why he had been driving the bus when he should not have been doing so and why it had been necessary for him to use such bad language in the proximity of passengers, as reported by a Miss Clark a member of the local council. The story was told once again and the inspector was given his chance to reply, which did not go down very well with the board, who after a very short discussion told the inspector that he would lose his position as a inspector and would be reinstated as a conductor.

With that, the late inspector just lost it and with a great deal more very bad language, told the board what they could do with their job and then, sticking up of two fingers towards the board with more verbal abuse in a manner that could only be taken one way, he then upped and walked out.

Once more Fred and I were standing outside Number 55 when up walked Madge and Tom, who apparently had the day off and suggested that we all do a bit more sightseeing. We all boarded a sightseeing bus, telling the conductor that we were on a busman's holiday.

He said, "That's okay with me," and joined us and knowing we were all bus folk, we received some special treatment. Along the route, as we were passing Lord Nelson high up on his column in Trafalgar Square, Tom dropped his bombshell by saying, but not looking at anyone in particular, "Would you be the best man at our wedding?"

The both of us, that's Fred and I, looked at each other and with great big grins looked round, saying at the same time, "Yes, I'd love to!"

And that's how Tom and Madge had two best men at their wedding.

Red and Green

On The Buses Number Three

It was our last day at Sutton (A), a London Transport bus garage, the ones with the large red buses. "We" were my companion, Jane and I, who were one of the many couples working at the garage as a crew. We recently had a bit of luck and found that our savings put us in the position of being able to put a deposit on a new three-bedroom house being built in Kent at a place called Wainscott, so we had put in a request for a transfer to the London Transport Country Services garage at Northfleet, near Gravesend.

This request had been granted and we were now doing the very late shift on the 164 route, which meant we could meet many of our friends from the garage, the firemen, the police and the late shift workers, all of whom relied on the last bus to get them home. We waited at Sutton Green to make sure we do not leave anyone behind and then on to Morden underground station. Being the last bus for the night, we always left with more than our permitted load, much to the inspector's disapproval, but making sure he was the last one aboard, we handed over our last big red bus to the maintenance staff and then Jane cashed in.

To get us home, we have our bikes but on this occasion and not like most cases, we walked up Sutton High Street doing a bit of window shopping, but not for the last time as we would return. Most nights we would find a bobby having a quick smoke and we always had some very friendly banter and then it was "Good night, mate" and on our bikes, as from the top the high street it was all downhill towards our last night in the home we had set up together.

We were all packed and ready for the drive down to Kent and our new home, so we made the best of the night and got some shut eye.

On our journey down to Kent in our very old Wolseley 12, we passed some very lovely views: old houses and many country pubs, making the journey a very happy one.

On our arrival we found the builder waiting for us with the keys. We had a good look round the house and garden and then started to unpack the car and soon after that the removal van arrived with our furniture. We did not have a lot; no carpets, no bed or curtains, but what we did have was all ours and paid for. What was left of the day we spent at the local pub and had a meal. We then laid some old newspapers on the floor, put the mattress on top, made the bed and spent a very happy first night in our new home. It was a good thing we were not overlooked.

On Sunday we got to know the other two neighbours, who had only arrived two days earlier. It was a new building site and our house was one of eight in the cul-de-sac, very nicely situated on the boundary overlooking farmland and very easy to get to work.

On Monday we reported as requested at eight o'clock to the area manager, who turned out to be a right old miserable person, all 20 stone of him. He did not have a good world to say about anything or anyone and all he said to us was, "You must get out of those blues and into greens as soon as possible," with a wave of his hand, which was meant to dismiss us.

But he did not know me because I stepped around to the side of his desk, taking and shaking his hand and saying,

"Thank you for your very kind welcome," and we both left him spluttering and unable to say anything.

We found our way to the canteen to get a cup of tea and a bun, only to be greeted buy a lot cat calling from its occupants, who were all in their greens, but once we explained that we were transferring we got on very well and found out that most of the crews were married couples or partners. It was Harry and Iris who took us to see the chief inspector, a Mr Green who we got on very well with, only to be told later that he had a eye for all the clippies.

The next day I was sent out to learn the routes and Jane had instructions on the new ticket machine and even did a short spell actually taking fares, but still in her blues, which made a talking point for passengers and the other staff. But after a day at the garage we both said how nicely we had been accepted and had a good felling about working at Northfleet.

Once again we reported at eight o'clock the next day, only this time in the company of other crew members. We all climbed onto a coach to go to the warehouse for our uniforms to be issued or replaced.

The company inspector said, "Okay, Leslie, you're driving. Don't worry, we will tell you the way."

That evening we both had a good laugh trying everything on.

On reporting the next morning Jane was sent one way and I was told that I'm to take over the next bus on the 480 route. New uniform, new route, and despite that, I found my way back to Northfleet safe and sound. That was when I found out that Jane had been doing some clippie work, so we'd both had a great day. That was when Mr Green told us that as from today we were on our own and tomorrow we would start at 6.30 on the 480s again, but we would be having a conductor to point out the do's and don'ts for the early workers' fares.

I gave Jane's hand a squeeze, saying, "See you at Erith, lovely."

The next day it was our first time to go out into the country. We started from Gravesend town where the inspectors have a booking office. We pulled up and the passengers started boarding. The inspector looked at his watch, saying, "Give it three more minutes, just to make sure we get them all," and with that he stepped into the coach, saying, "Anyone seen my missus?"

Someone from the back shouted, "She's still trying to cross the road!"

Everyone was now looking at his missus. The traffic was very bad and I could see that we would be waiting more than just those three minutes, so nipped out of my seat and waving my hanky, I managed to make a gap in the traffic and got his missus on the coach. She joined in with the rest of the passengers with a lot cat-calling and laughter and once they had all quietened down, she said to the inspector, "Don't worry, lover boy, I'll have your dinner on the table for you and anything else you may be looking for."

Once again the coach erupted and our friendly inspector had the last word, saying, "Don't get lost."

Just outside the village of Meopham, walking in the middle of the road because there were no pavements, were two old ladies, both struggling with two heavy looking bags. I stopped and opened the door and Jane said, "It looks like you could do with a lift."

They both said, "We would love a lift but we cannot manage those damn steps."

"Come on," I said. "I'll give you a bunk up."

The reply I got was, "That would be the first time in years, my lovely boy."

But I said, "Who's going to be first?"

By putting both my hands on her rump and one with good push, she was in. We had found out that their names were Mary and Mabel and it was Mabel who said, "I don't mind you being cheeky, just make sure you get a good handful, there's plenty of it."

Well, they did not stop talking until we got to their cottage and then they insisted on going down the steps backwards, telling me to get a good grip and with Jane making sure their bags went with them.

That's how it all started and on the return journey, standing outside their cottage, was the village Bobby, indicating for me to stop. He did not look very happy and once the coach door was open, he said, "I understand you have been molesting these to ladies and I have to make a—" but he could not keep it up and just burst out laughing, saying, "Thank you for your kindness in helping my sisters. Here are some goodies for you from my garden and when you get to the old folks' home, tell Pete it's okay."

Pete was waiting for us and I said, "Ray the bobby said it's okay," and with that he reached into the hedge, pulled out two rabbits and gave them to Jane, saying, "Be seeing you," and promptly disappeared.

It was our weekend off so with fresh vegetables and a roast rabbit for Sunday dinner, things are on the up and we were both very happy with our greens and were looking forward to our next trip into the country.

Keep Looking Out For On The Buses Number Four.

The Poodle's Revenge

On The Buses Number Four

Jane and I had been at Northfleet garage for nearly a year. We had settled in very well to our new home and working at the new garage was just great. I was also working part time for Pickwick Coaches in the mornings, taking the women and girls out to the farms for picking peas or seasonal fruits and sometimes to the processing factory.

On an early shift we had to bring them home and it was on one of these trips that I arrived early at the factory and got talking to Reg. He was one of the factory foremen, who was supervising the packing of some shipment orders for the next day's delivery when the second bus arrived. I had not seen this driver before and he made no attempt to say hello, so I just went on talking to Reg, who was showing me around the canning plant, but we could hear the girls calling so we both walked back to the parking area.

I was just about to move off when the foreman said, "That's funny, I'm sure that order was completed and now there are two boxes missing."

He must have realised what had been going on because he looked over at me, saying, "Would you please ask the other driver and the girls if they know anything about it? I had a quiet word with the driver, who's reply was just a string of very bad language with a "No!" at the end, and the girls they denied having taken them. I had a hard time getting off the upper deck, my face was covered in lipstick and how I retained my trousers I shall never know.

Reg the foreman said, "I'm sorry but I must ask you all to stay put while I make enquires with my staff.

It was about ten minutes later when two police cars arrived and both busloads of women started yelling and cat-calling, but it did not take them long. The police found the two missing boxes in the other bus's luggage bay. They had a few words with the driver, who got very aggressive, but it made no difference. They put the handcuffs on him and drove off with him in the back seat, still shouting his head off.

I found Reg and asked if I could make a phone call to arrange for a driver for the other bus. I told the girls and drove my lot back to the housing estate just outside Strood. I took the bus back to the yard where the boss man was waiting and said that if he took me to the factory, would I bring back the other bus? Not wanting to leave the girls out there, I said yes, but on the way I told him I would like to be paid up to date as this would be my last trip for Pickwick as I could not jeopardise my full-time job.

I got the other girls back and returned the bus and collected my outstanding pay. That was when Peter, the boss man of Pickwick's, said he did not like losing a good worker and that he would up the pay and could I find him another driver? Well, the driver I had in mind was a mate of mine and I knew he could do with the extra cash as his wife was expecting their first child, and on top of that the extra cash was buying a lot of things for our new home.

Jane and I had just had the weekend off and once more on our trusty scooter we arrived at the garage to start a middle shift only to be asked if we would mind doing separate jobs for the day, Jane on the Meopham run and me on the 701

Green Line route. Both jobs finished within ten minutes of each other so we said yes.

Now the Green Line service goes from Gravesend to Ascot or Sunningdale and takes just over three hours. I found the conductor, named Fred, had a drink in the canteen and walked down the yard. I found the coach, checked the seat and mirrors and Fred checked the blinds back and front and the off.

We went down to the town clock tower where we turned round and stopped outside the waiting room, as usual waiting to get the okay from the duty inspector. The last passenger on was a lady of about 45 with a small poodle. Fred very politely asked her to occupy the rear seat, which she did. The okay was given and we started off on time and everything was going to time – Dartford, Crayford, Bromley and Croydon, and we were heading for Sutton, my home territory. We had to stop at the Cock Hotel in Sutton to pick up passengers and who should be standing there, but two of my old Sutton mates waiting to take over their bus.

I moved the bus up a bit so that I could see them when I opened the door and called out, "Am I on the right road to Kingston?"

The look on their faces was worth a king's ransom and then they both climbed aboard slapping me on the back and asking me no end of questions.

"Sorry, lads, must keep the wheels turning. Jane and I will come to see you on our next day off," and with that Harry slipped a piece of ticket tape into my hand.

It was on our way to Ascot and we had just gone though Kingston when the poodle came up to the cab and started to bark at me. Twice more he managed to distract me and twice more Fred told the woman to keep her dog under control, so when the dog got off with some other passengers but not the owner, I said nothing and made sure the doors were closed very promptly. I carried on until I heard the scream from the back of the coach and someone saying, "Where's my little Fifi?"

I stopped at the next bus lay-by and one of the passengers said he had seen the dog get off at the last stop, so the woman got off, saying, "You have not heard the last of this!"

Fred got a couple of the passengers to give there names and addresses, just in case she made a fuss, and we drove on but that was not the end of it because someone at the back of the coach said the dog had left its calling card and the smell was that bad we had to ask the remaining passengers to move up to the front so we could open all the windows.

On our arrival at Ascot garage, we got lot of barracking from the garage staff, whose job it was to clean out the coach after the dog had left his unpleasant message behind.

It was while we were having our break that I remembered the piece of paper that Harry had given me. All it said was "Dream on, four o'clock, Ascot". I showed it to Fred, who was a betting man himself, and he said it might be worth a pound so we cut short our break so we could find a betting shop, which by sheer luck was just outside, close to the coach stop, so we both had a pound to win on Dream On.

On our return journey we met with a lot of unexplained traffic hold-ups and when we arrived at Kensington High Street we sat in one place for a good 20 minutes. Some of the passengers asked to get off as it would be quicker to walk and from then on we encountered traffic jam after traffic jam. In the end we made it to Dartford 35 minutes late and that's where the remaining two passengers got off.

Fred had a word with the inspector and when he saw the situation, he signed our waybill to enable us to run lights to Northfleet Garage. That's when Fred and I shook hands and I went to the canteen looking for Jane. I could see that our friends out in the country had not forgotten us because Jane was laden with goodies and even Pete the poacher had made sure we had a rabbit or two.

We had just made ourselves comfortable for the ride home when Fred came running over, saying, "Here you are, mate. Dream On came in at 20-1," and with that he gave me my winnings.

So that night we had fish and chips for our supper and I told Jane about meeting Harry.

Archie

On The Buses Number Five

I was about to start working my rest day as a driver for London Transport Country Service with the notorious Archie. Once the other drivers and conductors knew who I was going with that day, they all had a great time taking the mickey and shaking my hand and saying, "It's been nice knowing you. Have a humming day."

Now Archie had no regular driver as no one would work with him due to his appearance being very unkempt. He was about 50 years old, 5ft 10ins tall, truly very overweight and his uniform always looked as if he had slept in it and could do with a clean. Shaving was a task he tackled every new moon and he never wore a shirt or tie, only a black roll neck jumper, showing signs of all his previous meals down the front. He always wore white pumps, which were in a poor condition, and never any socks. As can be expected, his body odour was very pungent and all the drivers said they could not stand his continual humming, or as I found out later, his chanting.

Archie was a great believer in the arts of black magic in which he did a great deal of practising and the chanting was a big part of the ritual and the continual humming was the singing. On one of our breaks in the canteen, he also told me that he had made his bedroom at his lodgings looks like a temple as best he could, where until late into most nights he prostrated himself to his beliefs.

We had arrived late at the end of our journey due to heavy traffic in the town centre, in what we country drivers called "Indian country". In a red bus garage in Dartford, it's not worth getting out of the cab so I just looked through the glass panel and Archie give me the thumbs up and we went straight out again. It's a short run round the corner and onto the bus stop. The queue was a long one, far more than we could take, and I was just sitting and thinking that it was going to be a slow run up the hill with a full load when this good-looking women started to bang on the bonnet.

I slid open the small sliding window, not knowing what to expect, and before I could say anything she started to shout.

"Will you stop looking at my daughter?"

I was quite taken back for a minute but in retaliation I leaned out of the window saying, "It's not your daughter. She might be pretty, but she's far too young for me. I'm looking at you. I think you're lovely."

The whole queue started to laugh and that's when the bell rang and saved the day, so as we moved off I gave her a cheeky wave and blew her a kiss. She went completely scarlet. We only went a few feet and then we make a left turn into the main road and that hill and it was whilst turning that I could feel there was something wrong. The bus just swayed that bit more than usual and on top of that the engine was having a bad time of it. That's when I realised that Archie was up to his old tricks again, for which he had already been on report in the chief inspector's office, for overloading the bus and not issuing tickets but keeping the fares.

I don't think the passengers minded and you can understand why so many have a bus ride because although it's only about 200 yards long, it's a very steep climb and well worth the fare if you had to carry a lot of shopping. It's a narrow road, only two-way traffic, and looking up towards the top on the right you have a long brick wall holding back part of the hillside. On my left there was a footpath, on which the front doors of some very old cottages opened straight onto the pavement. But part of the way up, due to bomb damage, some of the cottages were missing and in their place three shops had been built: a newsagent and tobacconist, a chemist and a baker's. Due to our very slow run up the hill, there were no vehicles in front of me and because I was having to use second gear it was a slow climb. Coming towards me and the bus was a very large removal-type van taking up more than his share of the road.

At that very moment, the driver must have realised and turned towards the wall. His nearside touched the wall and then he swerved towards me and the bus. There was no doubt from the look on the van driver's face that he was in a lot of trouble. I checked the footpath, it was empty and I could only do one thing to get out of the path of what has now becoming a runaway van. I pulled hard over to the left, mounted the pavement and stopped just a few inches away from the baker's shop window, but the van just glanced off the rear end of the bus and landed on its side blocking the road completely.

On checking with Archie, we had quite a few passengers hurt, mainly the ones that had been standing in the lower deck and who had cuts and bruises. But those standing on the upper deck, who should not have been there at all, fared the worst and we had one women with a broken arm and another who had fallen down the stairs and was in a very bad state. That's when Archie's problems started because now the paramedics, inspectors and the police, with the fire and accident service in tow, had arrived. The police took me to one side and sat me on a chair, provided by the chemist, where I relayed my story to them. The inspectors were trying to talk to Archie but he kept walking away from them and doing a lot of shouting. I could only stay sitting as I was now shaking quiet badly and watch while the fire brigade had the job of cutting the van driver out of his cab.

He had also been very lucky regarding the accident, just a lot of blood from his head and a badly bruised leg, but he was accompanied by one of the police men, who put him in one of their cars and took him to hospital. It was my brother who arrived with the maintenance crew and what was to be the replacement bus, as he also works at the same garage as me but with the garage maintenance staff department. After some brotherly banter he went over to the inspector and said he was not happy about taking the bus away and would make arrangement for it to be collected by the tow wagon. Apparently he had also told the inspector that I was badly shaken up and not long after a car arrived from the garage and took me home with instructions for me not to report for work the next day.

Jane had a bit of a shock seeing me home so early and being escorted by a inspector, but that evening we had roast rabbit with all the trimmings (courtesy of Pete the poacher) and an early night. I was as right as rain the next morning and I even went by train to the garage with Jane, who still had to go to work, and I collected our scooter. It was while I was at the garage that I found out about Archie. Apparently he had given the police and the inspectors a very bad time of it, had landed up in the police cells for the night and was not released until midday. He was then taken to the garage by police car where he was told he had been suspended until further notice. At this he had just lost it and head butted the chief inspector, who was completely knocked out, and then smashed up his office and gave the police a bad time while being restrained. He was taken back to the police cells pending charges. Archie was once again released at midday two days later, was never seen again and never did attend court to answer the assault charges. He's gone but a lot of us miss him because he was a very colourful character.

It must have been eight weeks later that I received a letter summoning me to attend Dartford Magistrates' Court to give evidence regarding a stolen van and its contents. I asked to see Mr Green the head inspector and the union representative, a Mr Clark, at the end of my shift.

I entered the office and showed them the letter. I said if they were referring to the van on Dartford Hill, I did not know it was a stolen one. Mr Green said the best thing would be if he contacted the court or police and if I would call tomorrow. At the same time he should have some answers. I also made sure I would have union representative present at court and that there would be no loss of pay.

On the day in question I met up at the garage with the union rep and Mr Green and travelled by Green Line coach to Dartford terminus and then walked to the court.

There was a lot going on so we sorted out what court we were in and sat just outside. It was not that long before I was called. Standing in the dock I was having a good look round when the court went quiet and the members of the bench took their seats. It was a lady magistrate and after looking at her two colleges she nodded to the chap standing just in front of me, who then turned round and offered me a Bible and a card, saying, "Please read from the card to the court, unless you have any objections."

I did as requested and this tall chap stood up and looking at me, said, "Are you Mr Leslie James, employed by London Transport as a bus driver?"

"Yes," I replied.

He sat down and another man stood up, but this time I nearly burst out laughing because he was so fat, only about five feet tall and the wig he was wearing was far too big for his pin-sized head. His voice sounded just like it was coming from a tin whistle. How I managed to control myself I just don't know but I did and he asked me if I knew anyone in the court.

"Yes," I replied.

"Do you know anyone in the dock?" he asked.

"No" I replied.

He looked more than a little bit flustered and went very quiet. It was then that the lady magistrate said, "I think you had better rephrase your question.

Once again he was quiet, but eventually carried on, saying, "Do you recognise the person in the dock as the driver of the van that collided with rear end of the bus you were driving up Dartford Hill?"

"I'm sorry but I cannot be sure because the face I saw was one of complete concern and was slightly distorted. And being very busy myself at the time I had no time to take that much notice, so I have to say, no, I do not recognise the person in the dock as the driver."

The lady magistrate once again said, "I think you have gone as far as you can with Mr James and while you take counsel with your learned colleges, I would like to say to Mr James that I shall be writing to your employers regarding you're very quick action in avoiding a more serious accident on the day in question. Is there anything you would like to say?"

"Yes, ma'am. I thank you for your kindness and would it be permissible to address the person in the dock?"

She consulted her two companions and said, "I think that would be all right."

I turned towards the dock. The occupant looked so young and I said, "If you are the driver of that van, I would like to thank you for what you did in your attempt to avoid the bus, and good luck!"

The magistrate was smiling but said, "That will be all, Mr James."

All three of us left the court but waited outside. Mr Green had to see about the costs that the company had asked for.

I was standing near the entrance when someone said, "Thanks, mate."

It was the young driver, making a very hasty departure as his sentence had been a suspended one of 18 months. But his father, who had been in court, had been arrested for allowing a under-age person to drive the van and there was the question of the vehicle and whether its contents may have been stolen, so the company had to wait for its cost.

On our way back to the garage we had the time and started to talk about Archie and how he had avoided being picked up by the police. So far it was only Mr Green who said that he did not want to see him again, seeing that the last time he did so he landed up in hospital. But Archie had not forgotten that it was Mr Green who had arranged for his dismissal, as I found out later that he did a lot of his black arts mumbo-jumbo, all directed towards Mr Green.

Two weeks after the court appearance, our Mr Green was walking back to his office having been to see the maintenance manager. The garage staff weren't aware that he was walking between two buses and one of them having been refuelled, moved off, trapping Mr Green between them and causing him to receive some very severe injuries to his legs and pelvis. He once again landed in hospital and remained there for three weeks after having several operations.

It so happens that I'm once again working my rest day and it's a very late one and one of the maintenance staff gives me a lift down to the station. The train was already there and I flopped down on the first seat I could find. I could hear the whistle and a compartment door slam, but thought nothing of it, but something made me open my eyes and standing there was Archie.

"Christ, Archie, you did give me a fright. You could have coughed or something."

He did not speak for a good minute, but his eyes held me in my seat. They were completely black but shining.

"Tell me about Green," he said. It was not Archie's usual voice, very high pitched and I found myself telling him about the garage accident and the injuries that Mr Green had received.

Once again he just looked at me and then he said something in an unintelligible mumble and carried on, saying, "Damn him. I was aiming for his head."

He then seemed to relax and stepped forward, saying, "Would you mind if I shook your hand?"

I was taken completely by surprise but I did as he wished and he said, "You are the only one to have treated me with any respect and I thank you for that." With that he said, "Goodbye, Leslie," and was gone.

On our reporting for work the next day, Jane and I were once again told to report to the office only to find the new chief inspector and the police waiting for us. It was the police who informed me that Archie had been found in his bungalow that night, kneeling at his alter with his black candles still burning but completely dead. They then asked me to identify the body. Their request was okayed by the chief inspector and once again there was a ride in a police car to Rochester where Archie was resting.

I could not at first recognise him because for once in his life he was smiling. I could not help but think and wonder who he had met.

It turned out that Archie was an orphan, but also a very wealthy man and as it turned out, not such a bad one because he left everything to a local orphanage.

Good on you, Archie.

Jake

On The Buses Number Six

My companion Jane and I were reporting for work after having our scheduled two-day rest. We were earlier than usual that day as we had travelled by train as the good old Wolseley has finally given up the ghost and just would not start. So we now had no car and not knowing the times of the trains, we found we had time on our hands so we decided to walk from the railway station towards Gravesend clock tower.

As we passed the motorcycle shop showing a large range of scooters on display, it was Jane who said, "We couldn't afford a new car but we could just about afford one of these!"

So in we went, bumping into Ray the bobby, brother of the two sisters in "On The Buses Number Two". While looking around I could see Ray talking to the shop manager but thought no more about it until later when we had decided on one of the scooters and were talking to the manager about delivery, colour and taxing it.

It was he who said, "You know my brother Ray, the bobby, and my two sisters Mabel and Mary at Hartley Village, so Ray tells me. Well, just for you, I will come up with an offer you will like. Just tell me what model you like and see me tomorrow about the same time."

We could not wait but we made it at the same time and he called out, "Come into the office. I have put something together and everything is ready for you."

The paperwork was ready all I had to do was sign on the dotted line. It was a very good deal and just goes to show what doing a good turn to someone will do.

After a short lesson along one of the back roads with him as a passenger, he said, "You'll do. You can take Jane to work now," and that's how we became the owners of a new Lambretta 150 scooter in red and white livery.

As we drove into the garage, we were called into the front office and told that Mr Green wanted to see both of us. Well, no matter what we came up with, we could not think of anything we had done that would have us visiting the front office.

We knocked on the door and walked in.

"Ah yes, Jane and Mr James. Please come in and sit down."

Well, we had been asked to have a seat so it could not be a rollicking.

"I have two things to ask you," he said. "The first being, do you know of a Mr John James who has put in for a transfer to this depot as a fitter and has given your name as his reference?"

We both said "Yes" at the same time.

"He's my brother," I said.

"Good, that's one out of the way. Now the second thing is I've had a request from a crew for a change of duty for the next two weeks so that they can have time off to get married. Would you consider covering for them? It's the late shift on the Meopham route."

"That's no problem, Mr Green, we would love to help out and I understand that Mr and Mrs Williams are hiring a coach. I would like to be the driver and my services are free of charge."

On our first trip, who should we meet but Mabel and Mary, who had been shopping and that's how we got to know that Ray the bobby was away on a sergeant's course. On reaching the village, we stopped at the sisters' house and gave a couple of toots with the horn. It was just as well as most of the school kids who lived in the same area got off. It was on the way back that Mary and Mabel were waiting for us and started to tell us about Ray when this young bobby, about 20 years old, who was the temporary replacement for Ray, came over and asked what was wrong and why had we stopped, as they were not on the bus stop.

"It's all right, officer, I thought a cat had gone under the bus so I stopped and I was asking these ladies if they had seen anything. But just the same, if you don't mind, we will be on our way. I don't like running late." I called out, "Goodbye, ladies, and thank you!" And with that we carried on, but just to be safe, I reported the incident of my stopping for the cat to the inspector at Gravesend Waiting Room, but he already knew because the bobby had phoned it in.

Now as I have said before, this is the country run with its narrow lanes and not a lot of street lighting. We had finished our break back at the garage and were about to do the last run from Gravesend clock tower to Meopham. We collected the bus from the yard, down to the Gravesend war memorial, where we turn and head back along the High Street to the starting point and check in with the inspector, who gives us the nod when it's time to move off. But who did we have boarding first? Our new young bobby, Ray's stand-in.

Jane collected his fare and he sat just inside in the seat behind the driver's cab. Anyone boarding could not miss seeing him and some of the remarks made by the boarding passengers were not at very pleasant.

The inspector walked over and said, "I think that's all the regulars. Mind how you go," he said, nodding towards our very popular passenger.

I closed the door and with a wave to the inspector we went slowly through the town looking for and picking up as many of the late workers as we could.

Once we got out of the built-up area and into the country, we started dropping the passengers off outside their houses, or as close as we could. At the bobby's lodgings I stopped and let him off. I think the thank you was a bit quiet, but just the same it was a thank you. Jane and I both said good night, just that bit louder.

At the end of the village, we turned the bus around on the bus stand and had our 20-minute layover, resting on the two long seats. I think everyone was wishing Ray would hurry up and get back because even the pub had been closing on time. But even so, I think the landlord has been having a lot of late-night birthday parties.

Time to start back. We were already five minutes late and I was up in the cab pulling the starter and at the same time putting all the lights on, including the headlights, and who do I see? It was Pete the local poacher, who had been doing his rounds and was truly loaded down with three bags slung over his bike and his pockets bulging as well.

I quickly turned the lights off, opened the door and ran up to him saying, "I've just dropped the new bobby off in the village. You had better be on the look out."

"Blimey, mate, how do I get this lot to the old folks' home?"

You see Pete was the friendly poacher and he had permission from the local farmers as most of his swag went to the poorer villagers. But our new bobby did not know that. We both thought for a bit and then I said, "Sling your bike over the hedge and get in the back of the bus and sit on the floor."

We were now 12 minutes late and as we picked up the passengers, we asked them to sit in the front seats they all obliged. At the next stop one of the boarding passengers said, "That new bobby was up the road a bit."

This was one of these unlit bits of the route and as we went slowly around the next dog-leg of a corner, there he was, standing right in the middle of the road with his hand up and waving his lamp from side to side. Everyone on the bus must have seen him they all started to laugh, whistling and shouting.

I stopped, opened the door and said, "Can I help you, Officer?"

"I would like to have a look in your bus."

I was thinking hard as to what to say and how to keep him off the bus. It was then Jane who said, you're not coming on this bus with those muddy boots. What do you think would happen to me if someone slipped on the mud and made a claim against the company? I would probably get the sack and I cannot afford that so I'm sorry, not with your boots in that state."

He very reluctantly stood to one side and we continued on. It was about a mile up the road when I stopped outside the old folks' home and our friendly poacher slipped out the emergency door and disappeared, but he had left three rabbits behind and roast rabbit is one our favourites. I wonder how he knew.

As our friends got off, they all had a good word for us and we went back to the garage feeling very happy. I stopped at the top of the ramp outside the top office for Jane to cash in and handed the bus over to the garage staff. I had a few words with the night inspector about the policeman and his muddy boots and he said, "You did the right thing."

We know he likes rabbit, so when we saw him later as we were on our way home and he was standing at the top of the yard, I pulled alongside him, saying, "Just a little bribe," and gave him one of the rabbits and sped away on our scooter, both of us laughing.

We made good time getting home and so I was able to skin and gut the rabbits ready for the fridge before going to bed. It's nice here at Northfleet. I wonder what tomorrow will bring.

Well, the very next day we were once again on our country route and once again turning onto the stand when Jane said, "What do you think is wrong with that little girl?"

Well, we could both see that she was in distress and was limping badly, so as she came close, I said, "Can we be of help, young lady?"

With that, she started to cry and the pony she was leading was shaking its head and gave a loud nay. Jane took her into the coach and cleaned up her knees while I had words with the pony, who kept sticking his head into my pocket where I kept my apple. So in the end I just gave it to him and that's when Jane and Janet, who had told Jane everything, and I got to know that the pony's name was Jake. Apparently Janet had just fallen out of the saddle and could not remount so I lifted her up and once she was reseated, I told Jake to be a good chap and to see that Janet got home okay. The last we saw of them they were getting along very well.

Our next shift was an early start doing a split shift. That's where you take the early workers to work and later on you have the task of taking them back home again. Well, the first part was over and Jane and I were in the canteen having a snack when who should come in but Kath and Jack, who were on the same kind of shift as us and they joined us. That's when Kath said, "We are going to our granddaughter's gymkhana show. Would you like to come?"

Having made our minds up, we said, "We would love to," and so all four of us had a busman's holiday and made our way to the school by bus.

It was a very popular venue and the place was crowded, but even so, we made our way to the classrooms and had a laugh when we all put our signatures on the blackboard and tried out the small seats. Outside, the playing field was packed and the ponies and horses were being paraded round in a great big circle but that did not stop one of the pony's breaking ranks and pulling its owner with him and of all things, it was Jake who was making a bee-line towards me.

Once he got close enough, he gave that big nay and thrust his head into my pocket once more. I gave him my apple and I whispered into his ear, "Now you go out there and win for Janet."

He did just that and then we told Kath and Jack how it was that we patched Janet up and they told us that Janet was their granddaughter.

All four of us were back the garage to do the second part shift and that's when Kath said, "See you later. The fish and chip suppers are on us!"

About three months later Jane and I received a letter with two tickets for the Kent County Agriculture and Gymkhana Show. It said, "Kath, Jack and Janet would like you both to be their guests" and it was signed "JAKE".

The Jokers

On The Buses Number Seven

Once again, Jane and I were clocking on at Northfleet London Transport Country Services Bus Garage, where we were one of the many couples working as a driver and conductor team. Today we were on our favourite route which goes from Gravesend clock tower out into the countryside to Meopham and on this route we use the same type of coach as the Green Line service, which goes from country garages into London. The reason for this is that some of the roads are very narrow and have tight bends to navigate so the lower-built coaches will also not hit the lower branches of overhanging trees. Another reason it's our favourite route is because we get to meet many of our friends who live in or around Meopham.

We arrived at Meopham at 1.30, more or less on time due to a flock of sheep changing fields to graze in. We now had a layover of 25 minutes and so we called on our friends, as previously arranged, for a cup of tea and we ate our homemade sandwiches for our lunch. Our friends are Wayne and Mary Robinson.

Now Wayne also works at the same garage as us, only he just happens to be an inspector and he told us he would be riding with us as he was on the late shift. With that, we thank Mary and the three of us made our way back to the coach stand where we had left it.

On our arrival at the coach stand, all three of us just stood there looking at the space were the bus was meant to be.

It was Jane who spoke first, saying, "Our coats and hats are in the lock-up!"

The next to speak was Wayne. "You pair of jokers are the limit! Come on, where have you hidden the damn thing?"

It took a lot of talking to convince him that we were not joking,

We all walked back to Wayne's house and when we told Mary, she just collapsed on the sofa and could not stop laughing. Wayne phoned the garage first and then the police.

The policeman arrived on his push-bike and it just happened to be Ray, the village bobby, and a very good friend of Wayne's and ours.

He started the bantering by saying, "Don't you three like work? How much did you get for it?"

Some 15 minutes later the garage superintendent (who Jane had taken a dislike to) arrived and had a look at the empty coach stand as if he did not believe it, or any of us come to think of it.

He then said, "You had better come back with me and I'll get someone to make your report out."

That was when the Jane said, "We can make our own report out," in a tone that was not too polite.

He gave us a look, but got into the car, so Wayne got his ride to work just the same.

Well, that's how we got the nickname "The crew that lost or sold their coach".

The coach was stopped by the police on the A2 heading towards London with a crowd of "Ban the Bomb" hippies, who were enjoying a free ride. They were escorted back to our garage at Northfleet and once back on home ground, they just disappeared out of the rear coach emergency exit due to someone with the same sympathies for their cause who just happened to be looking the other way.

    I think that Jane felt sorry for them.

Blue Glove

On The Buses Number Eight

My name is Leslie James and having just recently left the regular army after eight years, I've taken up a temporary job as a bus driver for London Transport Country Services based at Northfleet, in Kent. Today I'm working my rest day and I find myself doing a very early morning walk along a country lane towards the railway station, thinking of the lovely warm bed I had left with my landlady still in it. I catch the 5.55 for London and the first stop, Gravesend, is my stop, which means a short walk to the bus depot. That is, unless a post office van or a police car spots me, as we always give them free rides and we get to know them late at night or first thing in the morning so they reciprocate.

Now this morning was very cold one and I walked at a brisk pace to keep warm, but I still had time to notice the tall trees and the hedgerows in their fresh coat of dazzling white frost making a wonderful picture. It was something low down in the hedgerow that made me take more than just a casual look towards the hedgerow and making me slow down. I could see what looked like a blue glove waving. I thought it was the wind blowing it but there was no wind so I took closer look and it wasn't a glove but a hand and from behind that hand came a very faint voice, saying, "Please, I need help!"

At first I was in a complete state of bewilderment and I took a step back, but once I was more in control of myself, I somehow managed to jump over the five-bar farm gate found an old chap and his dog laying under the hedgerow. I could see he and his dog were in a great deal of distress so I took my top coat off and wrapped it around him and his dog and put my gloves on his very blue hands. My first dismal attempt to use my mobile phone was a complete mess and on my second attempt I was more calm and more successful and I managed to pass a message on to the police and ambulance service.

The police arrived first, followed shortly after by the paramedics. While the paramedics were seeing to the old man, the police sergeant took my details and asked me the reason I was out so early and how I had spotted the old chap. He then said, "Thank you. I have your details and you may now carry on."

It was then that I realised that my mobile phone was still my top coat pocket and that was in the ambulance now so I asked the sergeant if he would be a good chap and phone the garage for me and to explain why I would be late. They did better than that and I arrived at the garage just three minutes late in the police car with all lights flashing and causing a big stir. It was a conversation piece at the garage for the rest of the day and I still in time to take the first bus out. After thanking the police crew and arranging for them to have a cup of tea, I drove out of the garage to start picking up all the early workers and any early morning policemen.

Three months to the day later, while signing on at the garage, I was summoned into the chief inspector's office, thinking, now what have I done?

I had no need to worry. You could see he was angry for having to start so early. He just looked at me when I walked into the office and, not saying a word, I looked over at his secretary but she was just a blank wall and was shaking like a leaf.

I said, "You did ask to see me?" and with that he went all red and barked something at me in a very unpleasant voice.

"Who do you know on the board?"

I said, "I take it you mean the London Transport Board?"

He started to say something but only managed to go an even darker red, banging on his desk with his fist. I waited for him to settle down and then replied by saying, "Surely it's my business and I would like to know why you are interested in who I may or not know on the board."

With that, he just lost it and went ballistic, shouting in a very high-pitched voice for me to get out of his office. I did just that, still not knowing what it was all about so I just put it out of my mind.

The very next day, once again while signing on, I was told to go to the chief inspector's office. I knocked on the door and walked in, saying, "You wanted to see me again?"

When he looked up I could see he was once again already very angry and I didn't think his secretary had moved from the spot she was in the day before, but today she was visibly shaking.

After a pause, he looked up, saying, still with that very nasty tone in his voice, "Who do you know on the board?"

It was my turn, so after a slight pause, I replied, "As I said before, I would like to know why you need to know."

How he controlled another outburst I shall never know, but this time he said he had been instructed by the chairman of the board to send me for training in Chiswick, West London to become an inspector. I thanked him for telling me and asked that he informed the board that I had no wish to be an inspector, and for his information and to the best of my knowledge, I did not know anyone on the board.

He did not say anything but just grunted and waved me out, and then all 20 stone of him collapsing back into his chair.

Since being at this garage I had made many friends with workmates and even with the passengers, mainly the ones on the country routes as we used a coach on this route and the cab was open to the public so anyone can speak to the driver. I always had something to say, a bit more cheeky to the good-looking females, or just being friendly and passing the time of day. Today I was on one of my favourite routes and was sitting outside the start point in Gravesend High Street.

The first passenger just happened to be Ray, Meopham's local village bobby, and his wife Kay, who are some of my friends. The next two passengers were strangers; very well-dressed gents who took up the back seats and asked for tickets to Meopham.

Now Ray and Kay asked me to dinner on Sunday, it being my rest day, to meet his brother and family, which I readily accepted because his wife Kay was a great cook. At the same time I asked him if he knew our two well-dressed gents on the back seat.

"No," he said, but he had noted that they are going all the way to Meopham and he would be keeping his eye on them.

It was when we got to Meopham, the end of the trip, that I had a big surprise as these two smart gents made a point of being last off the coach and the younger of the two said to me, "Are you Mr Leslie James? If so, could we have word with you?"

It was then that the penny dropped and I recognised the man in the hedgerow.

"My, my. You are looking a lot better than the last time I saw you and your dog," and with that, we both warmly shook hands and he introduced me to his companion, a Mr Robert McBruce, his solicitor, who handed me the suitcase he was holding.

He said, "Mr Martin McGregor would like to thank you for your kindness you have shown him and his dog and returns your great coat with mobile phone and gloves."

That was when Ray said, "Everything okay, Leslie my lad?"

I said, "Ray, I would like you to meet Mr McGregor," and they started talking as if they had known each other for years and Mr McBruce started asking me a lot of personal questions about myself.

It was Jane my conductor for this shift who told me, "The 20-minute layover has gone and we had better start our return to Gravesend."

Well, that was a very fast 20 minutes, so once more my two new friends took the back seat and off we went. One hour and 55 minutes later, on our arrival at the clock tower in Gravesend, I warmly shook hands once again with the two gents, who said they would be in touch.

I watched them walk towards a Rolls Royce, climb in and drive off towards the south. It was then that Jane told me they had been asking her a great deal of questions about me.

I made my way to the staff canteen at the end of my shift to save me cooking when I got back to my digs; it also gave me time to think about my meeting with McGregor. They were very nice gents but why all the questions? Well, any how, I had my belongings back.

Back at my lodgings, I must have dropped off in my favourite chair, as the banging must be my landlady knocking on the door and that meant a night of high passion, which I always found very much to my liking as she was one fine, shapely lady. So I put the two gents to the back of my mind for now, saying to myself as I opened the door, "Let the night's activities commence."

A week later I had arrived early at the garage and decided to have some breakfast before signing on as I still didn't like my cooking. I still had plenty of time but on signing the job sheet, once again I was told to report to the chief inspector's office. Now what had I done?

I knocked on the door and walked in.

"I understand you wanted to see me."

Once more he was sitting and just staring at the papers on his desk. I looked over at his secretary, who was once again of no help. He looked up and you could see that he was already in his usual state of anger and still in that very nasty manner managed to bark out, "Who do you know on the board? And this time you will tell me or you're sacked!"

Once again I replied, "As I have said in the past, to the best of my knowledge I do not know anyone on the transport board. As for sacking me, I can see no reason for you to consider such action towards me and I'll be taking the matter up with my union rep. Will that be all?"

Once again, between his spluttering, he managed to say in that same high-pitched voice for me to get out of his office.

Three days later, while at his home, he had a heart attack and died.

On this particular day, I had just finished my shift with Ann and was waiting for her as she had kindly offered to take me to her home for some bedroom frolics, when the day inspector called me over, saying, "This courier wants to see you."

After seeing my driving licence to confirm who I was, he had me signing for this posh envelope addressed to myself. To everyone's disappointment I did not open it there and then. Just at that point, Ann arrived and the ride to her home was a very precarious one for Ann's means of transport was a very old 350 BSA motorbike and I wondered if it would make the trip with the two of us, so I just shut my eyes and held on tight to that lovely body.

Eventually we arrived at her digs, for which I shall be eternally grateful to him above that looks after us. After Ann had had her lengthy payment with high jinks in her bedroom, she was a very happy lady and took me home. I had my shower and that evening I opened the envelope.

It was from Mr McBruce, asking me to ring him as soon as possible. Not a lot to say for a special delivery, I thought. I phoned him right away. He thanked me for being so prompt and told me that Mr McGregor would like to see me.

I told him my next day off would be my best bet and that would be this coming Friday, so it was agreed I would be at Mr McGregor's office in Sittingbourne on Friday at ten o'clock.

On Friday, walking down towards the railway station, I was miles away, trying to puzzle out why they would want to see me. In the meantime, I find myself sitting on the train to Sittingbourne still wondering why.

I arrived in plenty of time at the office and was shown into a very small, dimly lit office. The first to join me was a lady of about 60. I stood up saying, "Good morning".

She smiled saying she was Miss Clark, Mr McGregor's secretary and that he was sorry to be late.

I replied, saying, "I think it's my fault for being so early."

Just then the door opened and McGregor walked over, shaking my hand and saying, "I'm pleased you were able to come at such short notice."

He looked over at Miss Clark and said, "See if you can find out where Timber is, Jessie."

A few minutes later the door once again opened and all three of them, Jessie, Timber and McBruce, walked in and found chairs and now we were all looking at the boss man.

"Leslie, I have asked you here because our Mr Woods, who is our transport manager, has decided that he would like to retire at the early age of 75," which brought a smile to everyone present. He then carried on by saying, "Leslie, I would like to offer you that position."

I was flabbergasted. He must have seen my reaction because he said, "Take your time, Leslie."

After a very short pause, I said, "It sounds a very interesting proposition, sir, and I would very much like to take you up on your very kind offer."

There were smiles and handshaking all round and I was to start my new position on the first of the next month. That gave me just three weeks to hand in my notice at the garage and find new accommodation in Sittingbourne, which proved to be quite easy as knowing my new salary, not to mention the company car, was ample to cover most rents. I chose to rent a three-bedroom bungalow just outside Sittingbourne.

The three weeks soon went by and to be getting away from the landlady was bonus as she had started to talk about settling down and at that time I had no thoughts along those lines. I had already moved into my bungalow, had got to know the neighbours and arranged for a cleaner to come in twice a week and a gardener to look after the garden and keep the grass cut.

With my suit all nicely cleaned and pressed, I arrived for my first day's work at "the office" expecting to find Mr Woods "Timber", only to find Jessie telling me that he had been rushed into hospital two days before and the boss man was also under the weather as well. But she had been instructed to help as much as she could and would see that I had everything I needed.

I said, "Let's start with you showing me the offices and then the yard and introducing me as many of the office staff and members of the yard as we go and at the same time telling me what goes on. Maybe you could tell me something about yourself too."

My office proved to be to small and dirty with no windows and Jessie could see that I was not at all impressed.

"Is there anything I can help you with?" she asked.

"Get your pad," I replied. "First thing I shall be needing is a new office and if possible, red carpet, a larger desk, a new chair, one that swivels, and a bookcase. Some up-to-date books and government publications on road haulage, transporting perishable goods, road traffic acts for the past three years and all of Timber's records and papers. Plus anything that will help me do a good job running this place the McGregor way and then my way. And on top that, I shall need a secretary and I cannot keep calling you Miss Clark. Would it be all right if I called you Jessie?"

After a slight pause, she said, "That would be fine and as for a secretary, if you can leave that until tomorrow, I have someone in mind."

But Jessie had a funny look in her eye, which had me thinking, now what is she up to?

The next morning I arrived very early at the yard and introduced myself to a Mr Thomas in the dispatcher's office. Now our Mr Thomas was very unpleasant towards me and told me in not so many words that I was not welcome in his office. Nevertheless, I continued just taking note and could see that he was very uncomfortable with my presence. I did not like what I was seeing; the man was a big bully, using threats and a great deal of bad language towards his drivers and staff. The man was of an untidy and dirty appearance with it. I had seen enough and would have to make some changes and with that in mind, I walked back to my office only to find the boss man and Miss Clark waiting for me.

"Good morning, Leslie, he said. "How are things going?"

"Well, this not going to my way of working, sir, and that Mr Thomas is just a bully and his language is just disgusting. But I will sort something out in the very near future."

He looked over at me, saying, "Well, you're now in charge and I'm very sorry that we have managed to drop you in the deep end, so whatever you do, you will have my full backing."

"That's good to know, sir."

It was then that the police car arrived and Miss Clark showed a very tall sergeant in.

"Good morning to you, gentlemen. I'm sorry to have to say but I have one of your drivers in the car. I've arrested him for driving under the influence of drink or drugs and seeing that we have to pass your yard on our the way to the police station, I thought you might like to know that the vehicle he was driving is parked in a lay-by in Green Street."

He looked over at Mr McGregor, who pointed at me, saying, "He is in full charge as from this point," where all three of us burst out laughing.

The sergeant looked over to me, saying, "Anything you would like to say regarding your driver, sir?"

"No, sergeant. He knows the company rules regarding this situation, so no, just throw the book at him."

"Thank you, sir. There is, however, just one other thing. Sir, I think you had better look at the springs or check its load."

I relished what was being said to me, saying, "Thank you, sergeant. I'll do just that. And, sergeant, the next time you're passing, would you kindly call in to see me and have a cup of tea with me?"

I had been looking at the boss man, who did not look or seem to be very well. With the aid of the sergeant, we managed to get him seated. I asked him if he would like a cup of tea or coffee, but I could see he was not well at all so called Miss Clark and said, "Call his doctor and arrange for us to meet him at the boss man's house and we will take him home right away."

On our return from the boss man's house, Jessie burst out crying and then told me that she and the boss man had been partners for a long time and she felt very concerned about his health. It was then that some very loud knocking on my office door had both of us looking that way.

"Come in!" I said. It was Thomas, the driver who the police had charged with drink driving and who had obviously been let go.

"Yes, what can I do for you?"

"I need a job in the yard."

No sign of any please, just a very rude request.

"I'm very sorry, but I have no vacancies at the moment so I cannot help. All your pay, including any holiday pay and any papers, will be waiting for you on Friday at the front office."

After some very loud abuse towards us both, with also a great deal of bad language, he left, saying that he was going to see his brother the dispatcher and slamming the door as he went.

Jessie and I continued discussing the boss man, but at that point, there was more knocking on the door. It was Mr Thomas the dispatcher bursting into my office and in doing so, he just pushed Jessie to one side, shouting at her to get out of his way. Poor Jessie went flying, hitting her head on my desk and moving it two feet off its spot.

She groaned and lay very still. This time I was pleased that the other members of the staff were on hand and I just pointed at one, saying, "Call the police and the paramedics!"

The police arrived very quickly with blue lights flashing. I told them what had happened but in the meantime our Mr Thomas had done a runner so I gave them his address where they picked him up and charged him with GBH. They then brought him back to my office in handcuffs and I then told him he was fired and his money and papers would be ready for collection along with his brothers on Friday, if he was able to do so.

Now we were one driver down and with no dispatcher, but it did me a favour, in a way, as I would not have to fire him at a later date.

The paramedics had been and taken Jessie, still unconscious, to hospital for concussion, cuts and bruising and there she remained for the next five days.

The next morning, making an early start, I worked the dispatcher's office as we no longer had our Mr Thomas. Most of the drivers were pleased with the change and I found that the turnaround had increased. I noted that one of the drivers stood out from the rest, so without anymore to-do, I asked him if he could run the office without any bullying and bad language?

"That I can, sir, and I would love to take on the job."

"That's good." I replied. "As from now you're the man in charge," and with that I left him to it, saying, "Come and see me later in the day."

I was walking back to my office thinking that's one problem solved, when a police car pulled up alongside me and my friend the sergeant said, "Did you mean it when you said you could do with an ex-bobby to work for you?"

"That I did, sergeant. Come to the office."

The sergeant said, "This is a colleague of mine that has received his papers on medical grounds and I thought of you. I liked what I was seeing and said, "Tell me a bit about yourself.

He started by giving his name as Richard Archer, details of family and his address followed.

I said, "I need a security officer for the yard and offices and someone to check all vehicles in and out, and if you have another ex-policeman like yourself, I would like to see him and if he fits the bill, I'll take him on as well to help you. If you accept the position, I would like a report in writing within ten days of your recommendations on the security of this compound and offices. I am happy with what I have seen and heard and if you wish you may start this coming Monday."

Looking over at the sergeant, I said, "That's if the sergeant approves." We had good laugh and he agreed to start on Monday and he would have a word with another ex-bobby.

From that day things started to look up and for one thing, my chair had arrived and I had moved into the larger office, which had been the boss man's office and with the new desk and red carpet nicely fitted. Then I found that Jessie had pulled a fast one by introducing me to my new secretary, who just happened to be the boss man's granddaughter named Ruth, and she was a real stunner.

It was not long before I plucked up courage and asked her out to dinner and a show and things got better day by day. The business was showing a good profit and my continued improvement in office skills had paid off as we now employed a transport manager, another ex-policeman, allowing my promotion to general manager. As for the boss man, on doctor's advice he only calls in maybe once every two months after saying he would like to take things easier. He has taken Jessie with him and they now have a very nice cottage in the Wiltshire countryside at a place just south of Andover.

It's just over a year since Ruth joined us and seeing that she lost both parents in a car accident, I found myself asking the boss man, with Jessie in attendance, if I he would allow me to marry his granddaughter. They both looked at each other and Jessie burst into tears, but somehow they managed to say, "With our best of wishes, it's our greatest of pleasure to say yes."

It was just over a year later that we presented them with twins, a great-grandson and a great-granddaughter. The boss man was so pleased that we had named the boy Martin and the girl Jessie, that he insisted on handing the deeds to his old house in Sittingbourne over to us. When Mr Robert McBruce arrived a week later with papers to sign regarding the house, he let loose a bombshell by telling Ruth and I that he had also been instructed to have papers drawn up to hand the business over to us. We were both thunderstruck with this news, but at the same time it made us very happy to know that our future was safe.

Now I've been at McGregor's 12 years and in that time it has grown a great deal and is now one of the biggest distribution companies in the country. Ruth and I have also grown in family and we now have three fine boys and two very pretty girls. Well, we think so.

It was just after Christmas that an even bigger transport company approached me, asking if I would consider selling the company to them. We took a drive that weekend to see the boss man and Jessie and on showing him the paperwork, he just said, "What are you going to do?"

"I know that you made me the managing director and even handed the business over to me," I said, "but Jessie and I still consider it to be your company and I'm just looking after it for you."

"You, make up your own mind, my son. The company is yours and Ruth's. Jessie and I are too long in the tooth now so you do what you think best."

On our return drive home, we were both very quiet and did not talk about it until the next night as over the weekend the other company had increased their offer to £25million, plus a salary for me as a director on their board for five years at £200,000 per year. I accepted. The new owners were called Wickfords.

Book Two

This Way, Gentlemen

Wednesday – A Hot Day in June

As the train arrived at one of London's mainline stations, I picked up my old suitcase from the rack and waited for the crowd to thin out and started for the exit. I had only gone a few yards when a voice in my ear whispered, "Nice to see you, guvnor."

I knew the owner of the voice. I did not turn round, there would be no point, I would not see anyone. I'm Warrant Officer Leslie James, member of the SAS and as ordered, on my way to the Ministry of Defence office.

It was only about a mile to go but I just did not feel like walking to my destination, so I joined the queue for a taxi. Even so, not far from my destination I stopped the cab and walked the remaining few yards into the familiar building and went in by the side entrance. At the reception desk, after giving my name, rank and number, I asked for the duty officer. I was shown into a large room and was greeted by the station voice, Danny and Timber, both sitting comfortably in two large leather armchairs.

We got talking about what we had been up to, the weather, anything but what we anticipated may be in the pipeline for us, but not what we thought we had been called to the MOD for.

It was Timber who said, "No Knocker yet, guv."

It was as if Him up there must have been listening because the door opened and who should walk in, but Knocker, in handcuffs and with two MPs for escort.

"Good morning, guv and fellow countrymen. Meet my travelling companions."

One of the MPs stepped forward, saying, "Would you please sign my slip, sir."

"Do I have to?" I said jokingly.

"It would be better that way, sir, as I do not want to take him back."

The slip duly signed and the handcuffs taken off, Knocker once free turned to the two MPs and said, "Thanks, mate." And much to their surprise, shook their hands.

Apparently someone in the pub had made a remark about the woman in Knocker's company and he did not like what was said so Knocker hit him, not knowing that the man was in his local. His mates helped him up off the floor and then joined in setting about Knocker. Well, Knocker responded the only way he could by using his knowledge in the art of self-defence and unarmed combat and before the fight was over, he had managed to break three arms and a leg. That was when the police arrived and took him away saying he would be charged in the morning.

After a short spell in cooling off, he showed the desk sergeant his orders and after a few enquiries, the police called in the MPs, who made sure that he reported on time, so now the team were once more a team.

We all started to talk at the same time; we all stopped at the same time and then started to have a good laugh. It was a nervous laugh as we had all been there before and we had no idea what lay ahead of us. We did not have to wait long, a tall thin major of the Irish Guards made his presence known.

"I'm Major Maxwell and for the next few days, I shall be taking care of you," and then very politely said, "This way, gentlemen."

With an indication for us to follow him, we went along the familiar corridor, passing the door we had used several times before. We entered another large room which had one of the largest desks I had ever seen; it seemed to dwarf the two men in civilian cloths who were seated behind it. The major indicated that we should occupy the four chairs in front of the desk. We started to relax but a deep gravel voice soon put a stop to that.

"Good morning, gentlemen. Just to bring you all into the picture, I'm General Collins and on my right is Colonel Kodak."

Now the general looked the part – 6ft tall, sandy hair and a large whisky drinker's nose. With another look at Colonel Kodak, who was the complete contrast – tall, pale and very thin, looking as if he had never seen the daylight and had always been tied to a desk. The general carried on, saying, "We are, as you are, members of the SAS. There are two reasons for the request of your company, the first one being a very pleasant one for both of us. We have had the opportunity to look at your records and I must say they are outstanding, so making our first task that more pleasurable. The promotions I'm about to make are, in our opinion, long overdue and fully deserved, so without further delay, it is my privilege to say that as from this day you, Warrant Officer James, are promoted to the rank of lieutenant and the rest of your team, Sergeants Godfrey, Knight and Friend, are also from this day promoted to the rank of second lieutenant. May I be the first to congratulate you all."

The colonel and the major joined in and the drinks appeared.

Now Danny Godfrey was originally from London but now lives in Dover in Kent. He used to be a coal miner, was 5ft 10ins tall, slim, but worked out every day and was very fit. He had a very good sense of humour but did like his pint or two and the ladies.

Knocker Knight was from Petworth in Sussex. Once again 5ft 10ins tall, a very keen motorbike enthusiast and like Danny a very fit man, but he preferred wine to beer and he too was very much a ladies' man.

Now Timber was a different kettle of fish; 6ft tall, blond, blue-eyed and just as fit as the rest of us. He was a man of Kent, lived with his parents in Gravesend and started in the army on a two-year conscription service. After his eight weeks training he was posted to a unit stuck out in the wild blue yonder of Scotland and was made batman for a young, big-headed first lieutenant of the Royal Engineers. He did not like it and so applied for other duties and landed up in Herefordshire with the SAS. He has been a real asset to our team ever since. He liked a drink but was a one-woman man and her name was Anita.

The general, after talking to the major, turned towards us and said, "Time waits for no man, not even us generals. I'm sorry to say that the second reason for your being here will have to wait. Would you therefore join me for dinner tonight, say 2000 hrs?"

Coming from a general, that was no request, that was an order.

"The major will fill you in regarding dress and location. Thank you, gentlemen. See you at 2000 hrs."

The major once again said, "This way, gentlemen," and like a mother hen had us follow him a short distance to a hotel which overlooked Hyde Park.

"This is a bit better than the sergeants' mess," remarked Danny.

The major returned from the reception desk. "This way, gentlemen."

We took the lift to the 10th floor and were shown into two rooms, which very conveniently had connecting doors.

"Now, gentlemen, you are in no way prisoners to the hotel, but please refrain from going out. Room service here is very good and you don't have the bill to worry about, we see to all that. So you might just as well take full advantage of the situation. One more thing before I leave you, this hotel is known for its gentlemen's outfitters. It also has a very fine military department to which you are expected to take full advantage of as soon as I take my leave of you. You will arrange to have two uniforms made, one of which you will need tonight. You will also have two civilian suits made of your own choosing and make sure you don't forget to choose plenty of underwear, shirts, socks, shoes, and casual wear to travel in to make it look like as if you're going on a holiday. Just say General Collins sent you and we shall require one of our uniforms by 1900 hrs today, and then leave everything to them."

Just before 1900 hrs there was a knock on the door and in walked the major with an army of tailors, along with our new uniforms. Twenty minutes later and after a few adjustments, the major was satisfied and once more said, "This way, gentlemen."

Waiting for us at a side entrance were two staff cars. The major and I got into the first one and the three mere second lieutenants into the second. It was a short trip and we arrived at the American Embassy and we were escorted by two sergeants of US Marines and shown into a very nice room where a table was laid out with ten settings.

Right on the dot of eight, in walked the general with the colonel and a party of three in tow, with the exception of one very distinguished and well-dressed chap in a very expensive suit. The other two places were taken up by two uniforms, which we recognised as American Rangers.

In his deep voice, the general said, "Gentlemen, let's start the evening off by making same introductions. Major, would you do the honours?"

So we got to know the Americans, Colonel Winters and Colonel Sutton, both of the US Army Special Services. The other chap was no less than Congressman J J Oliver, who came with full powers from the White House.

The dinner was first class, as expected, but as always dinner and the chit-chat were soon over. The waiters cleared the table and served coffee. A large try of drinks placed on a table then they left very smartly under the eye of the major, but you could not help but notice the very large contingent of Military Police outside the door.

Danny whispered, "What in the name of Jesus have we got ourselves into this time?"

All four of us took a second glance at the door and then just nodded to each other.

The Americans, with their usual generosity, had been handing out the Havanas and the room soon filled with blue smoke. The general banged on the table and the buzz of chatter stopped.

"Gentlemen, I'm sorry to say it's time for business to commence. Major, be so good as to show our guests where to sit. We, the team, were shown to one end of the large round table, with the others at the other end and the major standing behind the general. The general, now standing up, looked around the table and waited for everyone's attention.

"Before we continue, I must point out that what we are about to discuss is strictly top secret and must not be discussed outside of this room. If any person or persons should approach you on the subject we are about to discuss, you will have them arrested at once." Once more seated, the general said, "We have been asked by our American friends to help out with a situation that has been a problem to them and has recently started to be a problem to our own government. Now prior to this meeting, both governments and their special service departments have got their heads together and decided on the following plan of action. This kind of action, being unfortunate, is in their recommended and considered opinion, the only way out of this situation."

The general looked down to our end of the table. "You, gentlemen, with your previous experience and expertise, are simply here because you are the best we have to offer and we shall need the best to carry out this recommended task."

The plan was then explained to us by Colonel Kodak, with a lot of unnecessary detail and could have only been put together by a load of Boy Scouts going on a weekend camp. Not a word about the many preparations required, the organising of the combined services to get you to a start point, special equipment and specialist personnel that may be required, and then the training of body and of mind for those who were taking part. Whoever these scoutmasters may be, they just had no idea of the amount of planning, the training, and a great deal of very hard work it takes to set up one of these operations. What goes on out there, the tension, the fear of just being there, knowing you would not be made very welcome if things went wrong.

One look at the lads and I knew the same thoughts that I was having was going through their minds. No one said a word, but all eyes were on us, "the team".

I stood up, feeling very conspicuous with all eyes now on me.

"Sir," I said, "I would appreciate, with your permission, to have a few moments with my team. On our own, if that could be arranged."

"Granted," said the general. "While you are away discussing what you have heard, remember that both governments will give you full support if you should decide to take on this operation."

The major once again took us in charge. "This way, gentlemen," and with our escort of MPs, went to another room just along the corridor.

We all flopped down into the large leather armchairs conveniently situated around a table, which was laden with drinks. It was long five minuets later and I could see it was up to me to make a start.

All I could come up with was, "What a load of crap that was. So come on all you second lieutenants, what about some ideas?"

The response was not that of a newly appointed officer or gentleman of HM Army, but it did do the trick. Timber was the first to reply.

"Their plan, that's for sure, is a one-way ticket to hell and I understand that the beer is not that good there. I'm sorry, it's not for me, guv."

We all agreed that the plan, as told, was doomed from the start and like Timber, we just did not want anything to do with it.

"So what's it to be?" I said looking at them all.

Danny said, "I'll give it ago only if we can make our own arrangements."

Knocker said, "I'll go along with that."

This was the opinion of us all. We all sat thinking of what may lay ahead and still no one had had a drink. I walked over to the door, turned and looked at them. All three gave me the thumbs up. A knock on the door and the major, who must have been waiting just outside, stepped into the room.

"Well, gentlemen, I see you have not had a drink and seeing that we still have some time, will you join me? My treat!"

"You're a gent," said Timber. "We could all do with one."

"May I join you, then?" said the major.

After we had had a couple, the major, once more standing up, said, "This way, gentlemen. If you gentlemen would be so kind as to follow me."

With our escort of MPs, we once more entered the smoke-filled room. The general, looked very flushed and for one moment appeared to be lost for words, but very quickly recovered his composure. We all reseated in our same places. The general, now more composed, looked down the table at the team.

"Well, gentlemen, what have you come up with?"

I stood up and said, "Sir," and at the same time looking at the three Americans. "My team and I have all come to the same conclusion. With all respect to the heads of departments of both governments, the way the operation has been put together and presented to us and we cannot see how it can be a success. We are of the same opinion that your plan is doomed from the start. This being the case, we regret that we have no other option but to decline."

The room went very quiet; you could here a pin drop. I waited about 30 seconds and then still standing up, I addressed the other end of the table.

"Sir. However, we do have a proposition." You could actually feel the relief in the room. "We suggest that another meeting be arranged and that I and my team be at that meeting. I think we are in a far better position to give some vital support to the planning and we can make sure that the plan will fit in with our way of working. We shall still need the full cooperation of both governments. Sir, I hope this will be to your approval."

The general, standing and looking much relieved, said, "Gentlemen, I can see nothing wrong with what you propose. Thank you."

He then, with Colonel Kodak in tow, walked down the table and shook hands with us all. He was then joined by the Americans and the major. Once more the general knocked on the table, and looking towards our end of the table, said, "Gentlemen, on behalf of the British Government, and I feel sure our friends from America, we will see to it that every assistance shall be given. Once again, thank you. Lieutenant James, Lieutenants," said the general, "the major will take care of you from now on and I must ask your forgiveness once again as I must leave you to make my recommendation to my superiors."

With that our friend the major, after speaking with congressman, once again in his very polite voice said, "This way, gentlemen."

As far as we the team were concerned the meeting was over. On the way back at the hotel, the major said, "Have a good night, gentlemen. I'll see you at 0800 hrs tomorrow.

Dress uniform. You and I have a great deal to do. I will explain tomorrow on the way to our destination."

The next day, promptly at 0800 hrs, the major arrived at the side entrance with a large limo and asked Danny to drive.
"We are going to Aldershot and when we arrive there I shall hand you over to the camp QM who has been told of your arrival but nothing regarding the future and you will not enlighten him in any way. Now then, any item of kit or weapons you require you must ask for, and do not leave there until you are satisfied, and make certain you get a list of what you have requested as this will all be crated up and waiting for dispatch at your request. Your QM visit should only take about one hour and once you have completed your business there you are to go to the officers' mess and ask for me. Wait for me in the bar. You will probably have time for one drink."

It was very hot outside and the QM had been a pig when he realised that we had nothing to tell him. The thought of that drink sounded good to all of us.

"Hang on, Timber," said Danny.

"It's the governors privilege to set them up, as he out ranks us," said Knocker.

We all had a good laugh.

The lager was going down well when Knocker said, "Drink up, chaps. Here comes the major."

As he approached, he indicated for us to remain seated. He pulled up a chair and joined us.

"Well, gentleman, the meeting you suggested has been arranged for 1700 hrs. We still have some time, would you allow me buy you a drink?"

It was then that the QM walked in and made his way to our table.

In a very loud voice he said, "I might have known, Major flaming Maxwell, that you would be involved with this lot."

Now everyone in the mess could not help but look our way.

"Come on. What's on?" continued the QM in that very loud voice.

The major, standing up, went very red, and walked to the door. Coming back with two MPs, he showed them a card and they both stood back and saluted. The major then turned to the QM and said, "Sir, would you please accompany the MPs, you are under close arrest."

The QM's face went red with anger and that was the last time Aldershot saw anything of him.

"I'm sorry, chaps," said the major, "but I have gone right off the idea of a drink. Would you kindly come this way, gentlemen."

We all went to the door and the major, pointing to the limo, turned to Danny and said, "Would you be the driver again? Turn left out of the gate, take the third exit out at the roundabout and I will direct you from then on."

It must have been the old garrison church that we arrived at. We parked alongside five other staff cars; two of them had American MPs for drivers. The major called the other drivers over and pointing to the limo said, "Go to the sergeants' mess. I've arrange a meal for you. You are to wait there until called."

The only other personnel in the area were the ever-present MPs and they must have been 50 yards away. We must have been very late and we could see the major explaining the QM incident to the general.

The general said, "Let's go in, gentleman."

Once again the large table and the other occupants of the staff cars were already seated. In all, there were three colonels, the two Americans we had already met and the English one was Colonel Kodak. The forth member was Commodore Griegson of HM Submarines. The general and the major were seated not at the table but within earshot of what was about to take place.

Colonel Kodak stood up and turned to the general and asked permission to carry on. The general said, "I would like to make just one suggestion, which is for the duration of this meeting, you gentlemen at the table forget your rank and act as a team."

"Yes, Colonel, please continue."

Colonel Kodak, still standing, said, "Gentlemen, as you know we are here to convene a plan of operation to replace the one that was found to be unsatisfactory. A plan that will be agreeable to both governments and to our friends seated with us."

The talking went on for about three hours before I and the team agreed on a plan that was, in our belief, a working one and on the understanding that we be informed of any change.

Colonel Kodak said, "Thank you, gentlemen. Your knowledge of this kind of situation has opened my eyes and I have gained a great deal from this meeting."

The Americans, Colonels Sutton and Winters, said, "Thank you and we are also very impressed with you and your team's knowledge and planning skills."

Colonel Kodak then turned to the general and said, "I think that just about brings the meeting to a close, sir."

The general, who had been a very interested participant, said, "I thank you all for coming and I think it's time we got started on what you have agreed on. Major, let's get back to the mess, I'm thinking we could all do with a drink."

The major said, "Everything has been laid on, sir. I'll call for the transport."

Back at the mess the major whispered to Danny, "You may drink. I have arranged for a driver to take us back to London."

"You are a gent, sir. You think of everything."

The dinner turned out to be yet another meeting regarding the future operation, as well as some surprises. Apparently we were to do our training in the USA at a Special Services camp, Fort William in Texas. The terrain in the area being somewhat similar to what could be expected at a later date. We were to report to the officer of the day at Fort William by 2359 hrs, 21 days after departure from the UK. This would enable us to have a spot of leave before reporting for duty.

Twenty-one days later at 2330 hrs, the two taxis dropped their passengers of at the barrier of Fort William, Texas, USA.

All four passengers were still dressed in their very colourful holiday attire,

It was a dark night but the camp entrance was like a Christmas tree. Lights were blazing everywhere.

"Take it easy, lads. We are being watched by the sentry who just happens to be one very big snowdrop. It's time to start work, my merry men. I think we had better report in."

We walked up to the guard and I said, "Good evening, sentry. Lieutenant James and Second Lieutenants Godfrey, Knight and Friend. We are members of Her Majesty's Armed Forces from England. We are reporting as ordered and we wish to see the officer of the day as soon as possible, please."

The guard on the gate had a long hard look at us and then called the officer in charge of gate control out from his office.

"Sir, I think they are Limeys and they are asking for the officer of the day."

The officer must have been told of our arrival and he very politely said, "This way, gentlemen," and showed us into his office.

Once inside, he said, "Your papers please, gentlemen."

He looked them over for the second time, before he made a phone call.

"They have just arrived, sir. Yes, sir."

That was the end of that conversation. He turned to us and said, "Nice to have you at Fort William, gentlemen. Transport is on its way."

It was not to long before we heard the transport pull up outside. Surprise, surprise, as in walked the major, and in uniform at that.

He shook are hands with all of us very firmly and said, "It's good to see you again. I trust you all had a pleasant trip out? Mind you, I did start to get a bit worried at 2300 hrs. Now, if you would be so good to come this way, gentlemen, I will take you to your quarters," which proved to be a block of 20 bedrooms and all as good as any hotel.

We could all have our own rooms. It also had its own gymnasium and a planning or chart room large enough to seat about 25. Out back was another smaller block, which proved to be two more bedrooms and a well-equipped kitchen.

"You will find a jeep parked outside in the morning. Use it to get to your bearings of the camp and I will see you in two days' time. Just one other thing. Please restrict yourselves to the camp for the time being. From now on the sergeant," indicating a tall top sergeant standing just to his rear, "will take care of you as I have been recalled back to Blighty and leave tomorrow on the night flight. So good night, gentlemen."

We all expressed our thanks to him for taking good care of us.

The major arrived the next morning, once again with the top sergeant, and they both set to and helped us organised our little part of Texas. In a very short time they had the chart room looking the part.

It was Danny who stepped forward and said, "It will not be the same without you, sir," and with that we all shook his hand warmly and thanked him once again for all he had done for us.

The major continued, saying, "The sergeant has been given full authority to see that your every wish be granted. It's been a pleasure to meet you all and the best of luck. Please look me up on your return.

"Now before I go, lieutenant, I would like to have a word with you."

Once out of earshot he continued. "I'm going to give you a number for any emergency that may arise and I would appreciate a coded report once a day, starting right away.

So our friend the major left us. We all felt as if the umbilical cord had been cut with dear old Blighty. We turned to the top sergeant.

"Well, Sergeant, what's your first name?

"Top Sergeant Bartholomew MacDonald, sir. But I'm called Mac."

"Right, Mac it is. Now, Mac, the first thing, 0800 hrs tomorrow, what we shall be needing is fatigue dress and a look around the camp to the parts where you hang out. We have to get to know how you tick if we are to work with you."

Mac hesitated and then said, "Would you mind if I took the jeep as his billet is on the other side of camp?" A few more questions to Mac and a phone call to the officer of the day soon had that sorted out and Mac now billets with us. This turned out to be a very good move on my part as Mac was a very good source of information.

At 0800 hrs the next morning, after a shower and breakfast, I said, "Okay, what's first, Mac. It's over to you."

The QM stores proved to be the first stop. We received three sets of fatigue dress and a bonus of two pairs of American-style para jump boots with compliments of the QM himself.

Now for a tour of the camp, we left the driving to Mac as they drive on the wrong side of the road out here, and we asked him a lot of questions, all of which proved very helpful at a later date. It was then that I decided to call on the camp commandant before calling it a day.

I knocked on the door and walked in, asking the only occupant at the desk in the centre of the room to see the camp commandant.

"Someone to see you!" yelled the desk jockey.

"Send him in," replied a voice from the outer office.

I walked in and saluted. Who or what rank the person was was also hard to tell, as he was in a state of undress and mumbled, "Well, what is it? I'm kinda busy right now."

Still standing to attention, I explained who I was and that I and my team were there at the request of the American government and that Congressman J J Oliver and Special Services Colonels Winters and Sutton would verify my statement.

He stopped whatever he was attempting, looking at me with a blank expression. It was then that I suggested that he make a few phone calls and I would call again the next day at his convenience. To which he replied, "You had better make it 1500 hrs tomorrow."

I saluted and walked out, still not knowing his rank or his name. At the jeep I said, "Let's get back, I need a shower."

After explaining it to the lads, Danny said, "What a wanker!"

It was then that Mac said he was Captain Dawson, who hadn't made the promotions list last year and made it hard on everyone, as well as himself.

"I'm going to my room for that shower now. Let's call it a day."

It was great just standing there letting the water cascade down. I even thought about singing, but thought better of it. But all good things must come to an end. I could hear one hell of a commotion going on outside when Danny came in saying the camp commandant was outside with half the camp's MPs and he was asking for me.

"Tell him I'll be out as soon as I can get some clothes on."

I walked into the chart room dressed only in a towel wrapped around me to find Mac, the lads, two MP sergeants and the captain.

"Sorry to have kept you waiting, Captain. As you can see I came as soon as I could. Would you mind coming through to my quarters so as I can make myself more respectable and we can talk at the same time?"

"Well, Captain, I gather you have been in touch with the congressman and Special Services, so what can I do for you?

"Sir," the captain was looking very worried and then after a short pause said, "I have been informed very strongly by the powers that be that I'm to make available every facility the camp has and anything you need, I'm to see that you get it." Another short pause. "Regarding this morning, sir, I was out of order earlier. Would you please forgive my rudeness?"

"Well, captain, it's my time to eat humble pie. I'm Lieutenant Leslie James of Her Majesty's Armed Forces, so you see you have no need to call me sir. I and my team are here at the request of your government. I cannot tell you why at the moment but no doubt you will be informed at a later date. As for yesterday, I cannot remember a thing, so how about I get Mac to arrange a dinner so that we can get to know each other and we can start again? Let's say tomorrow, about 2000 hrs."

We then joined the rest in the chart room. The captain said, "I'll leave the two sergeants with you. They may come in handy. I looked over at Mac, who gave a gentle nod as if to say, yes. I thanked the captain and reminded him of the invitation, which seemed to please him and we parted good friends.

"Everyone in the chart room please, gentleman. I'm sorry, but it's back to work. Now, Danny, Timber and Knocker, you three can start earning your keep. Take the two sergeants. Sorry, sergeants, we will get to know you better later on. We shall need by 1500 hrs tomorrow three more jeeps and two of them 10/12-seater cross-country vehicles, all fully equipped for cross-country work, extra cans of fuel and a good mechanic to take care of all the vehicles. Make sure he has tools and spare parts. The next thing is a wireless set, with capabilities of a 200-mile radius and man-to-man handsets, one per man and an operator who knows what he's doing."

I called for Mac. "Go and see whoever you must and get some cooks and get the kitchen working. We have a dinner to organise for tomorrow night. And, Mac, ask the QM if he would give us the pleasure of his company. And, Mac, see to it that the cooks have some knowledge of English cooking and have them draw a field kitchen and supplies for ten days and make sure it's no rubbish. Well, don't just stand there. There's work to be done!"

I had been sending my daily reports to the major and in response, a sealed package had arrived that morning so while the rest were out digging up the stores, equipment and personnel, I was able to have a quick look at some of the details and location of our intended operation and started working out some sort of plan for when the team and I could get together to work things out to all our satisfaction. This has been our strong point so far, plan and work together, and it works.

The next day they had all been working very well. I had seen the cooks and they seemed okay. I told them what was expected and of the dinner that night. Mac had also arranged for a cleaning party and the kitchen was taking shape. Danny came into the chart room and said that all the transport and other equipment I had asked for was outside for me to check over.

They had done very well and I was pleased with the result.

"Mac, get everyone into the bus and have some MPs guard the place. And tell whoever's in charge that we can be found at the sergeants' mess for the next hour…

"Beers all round please, barman. And have one yourself."

We managed to find a corner and then I thanked them for the hard work they must have put in. We spent the next hour in a happy environment, but back to work we went as there was still a lot of work to do.

"Mac, Timber, will you please come with me."

I headed for the chart room and made sure we would not be overheard or disturbed.

"Timber, you know what to do."

Timber made his way to the door.

"Mac you are a very intelligent chap, as your attitude towards us Limeys shows. You have already put two and two together and have a good idea why we are here. I ask you to say nothing to anyone of what you may have come up with and if anyone should get inquisitive, please report them to me. And, Mac, rank has no privileges. Now, Mac, for tonight a slight change in the menu, I want you to arrange for a barbeque-style meal so that we can be free from anyone being close by. We shall do our own cooking. Only my team, the QM and camp commandant are to be allowed in the building tonight until I say otherwise. Yourself and what MPs you need are to be on guard. I'll leave you to make the arrangements."

The same day at 2000 hrs, Mac had done very well. The MPs were checking everyone's ID and the rumpus at the front door was because the camp commandant had no ID on him and they would not let him in until Mac okayed it. As they arrived, I introduced them to the team.

The evening went very well and having had permission from the major I informed our two guests that our presence in Fort William was at the request of the United States Government and the British Government, and we were there to polish up on our training for a operation that had become rather urgent. But no dates or locations or any other information was passed on. They did look at each other for a long time and even shook hands. They both came to me and shook my hand, as well as the rest of the team.

"Gentlemen, I'm sorry to have to say, but we still have a lot of work to do tomorrow and it's well passed midnight and we do need our sleep. We thank you for coming. Mac has laid on transport for you. It was a pleasure meeting you both."

0800 hrs the following day. Our equipment from the UK had arrived late the previous night. After myself and the team had made our check on our individual requirements, in my case the Lee Enfield No. 4 Mk. 1 (T). I called for Mac.

"You will find two crates in the chart room. Have them loaded with the rest and I would like everyone and all equipment ready to go by 0900 hrs."

"Yes, sir," he replied. "May I have a word, sir?"

"Sure, Mac, go ahead. What is it?"

"How about taking me along with you on this exercise?"

I was taken aback by his request and looked over at the Lads, who made out that they had not heard. I could understand their feelings as we had always worked as a team.

"You will have no worries about the camp. Sergeant Morgan will see to that, sir."

"Okay, Mac, I'll give you my answer once we get to our destination."

At 0900 hrs and I looked over at Mac and said, "You have the map reference, I would like to get to our destination as soon as you can, so let's get rolling."

We made very good time and camp was soon set up, radio contact with Fort William had been established. The team and I made preparations to get on with our departure. I called Mac over.

"Okay! You can accompany us but remember, we cannot carry you. Sergeant Morgan, you are to take over Mac's duties and remain here until we return. No one is to leave. If you have a problem, call me on the radio. But do not leave this point for any reason."

We used one of the track vehicles for the first 20 miles, debussed and sent the driver back to our camp. Then we started out across the hard terrain towards the mountains.

We had been going for about three hours; we had no problems with Mac, he had been keeping up very well. We found a spot to make camp in.

I said, "Right, now that we can talk without others disturbing us." I looked over to Mac. "Mac!" I said. "I must have been mad to let you come with us but now that you are here I must point out that anything you hear or see is strictly top secret and must not be repeated. Do you understand what I'm saying?"

"Yes, sir. I have no problem with that."

"Okay, then. Let's get on. We can now have a look at the situation we have to deal with. Danny, would you spread out the map? I have already had a look and have come up with some ideas."

I explained what I had come up with. They all had a look at the map and details of what needed to be accomplished. Danny made a good point, regarding the target area; the actual location of the house we were to target was in a depression and showed promise of good cover.

Then Timber said, "How about carrying a bit less equipment? We could make better time and it looks like we shall need it. Most of the time we are out there, we will be in the open and we shall need all the help we can muster."

"What about it, Knocker? Got anything to say?"

"They are both good points, guv, and I go along with it."

"Right, let's rest up for a hour and then push on. You have to get a bit of training in. I don't want any passengers in the team."

The comments to that were unprintable.

"That, gentleman, has qualified you all for a court martial."

More comments followed.

Mac was bursting his sides laughing. You Limeys always like this?" he managed to splutter out.

"We have our off days," said Danny, and with that we all fell back and rested.

We all lay there talking and the hour soon passed. Once more we made tracks and headed for the mountains. We stopped and carried out various actions to stimulate any situations that may occur at a later date. It proved to us that we had not forgotten anything and Mac had slotted in with our ways and we all said how glad we were to have him along. Our little exercise had just made us that bit sharper.

I looked around the team and said to myself, we are ready.

Danny said, "How about slipping back into camp without them knowing. Give us a bit of fun and that bit more training. It would be good to see their faces when we turn up for breakfast."

We had been out for four nights and it was about 0500 hrs on the fifth day when we stopped about 500 yards from the base camp. We could see the sentry quite clearly getting into camp; shouldn't prove too much of a problem. About 300 yards out we dropped off our packs, retaining our weapons and very quietly made our way back to camp, slipping into our tent and leaving a note pinned to the flap requesting five English breakfasts at 0700 hrs.

Someone must have told Sergeant Morgan of our return because at 0700 hrs the tent came crashing down on top of us. But waiting outside, all laid out, was our five English breakfasts – "American style". We all had a good laugh and got stuck into our breakfast.

I called Sergeant Morgan over.

"About 300 yards north of here you will find our packs. Send a jeep and two of the lads to collect it, please. Then, I want someone to drive us back to camp. You will remain here in charge. Clean up the site and follow on. No need to rush, but on return have all vehicles checked and refuelled and see that all stores are replaced. We leave once more in a day or so. I'll leave everything to you."

We, the team and Mac, had a good trip back to Fort William. Mac told the driver to get something to eat and to report back to Sergeant Morgan as he would need the extra vehicle. With that we all made a bee-line for the showers and arranged to meet in the sergeants' mess for a beer.

I sent my report to the major, only this time I added, "Ready to proceed. Await orders".

It was five days later when the major, General Collins and Colonel Kodak arrived. The major suggested that the other rooms be prepared as others would be arriving in the next 24 hours. Our "hotel" now had a full complement of personnel and you could not move without bumping into an MP. This was keeping the cooks at it all day.

The general called the major over and was heard to say, "Have the meeting set up for five days from now. That should give everyone time to get here and settle in. In the meantime, I would be pleased to have drinks with the team. About 1500 hrs would be about right."

We had all made our way into the chart room and as usual, the general arrived on the dot of 1500 hrs.

"Nice of you to come, gentlemen. Have you all got a drink? Good. Then lets sit down. Now, gentlemen, there is no other way of saying this."

I could not help looking at the lads and they were all looking at me.

The general went on.

"I've come to an agreement with our American friends that a observer from their Special Services is to accompany you on the intended mission."

It was Knocker who summed it up for the team as he mumbled, "Bloody Hell."

The general looked and paused, but then carried on.

"I'm sorry and I will understand if you require more time for training. Major, would you ask our friend to come in?"

The major opened the door and in walked Mac in full uniform, and a Rangers major at that, and who also had a bloody great grin on his face.

The team stood up as one and said, "You old bastard! That's why you wanted to go on the exercise!"

With that we all shook hands with him and said welcome aboard.

The general gave a cough.

"I take it, gentlemen, that you have no objections to your new recruit? Now I point out the obvious. The major out ranks you all and will only be an observer but he will respond to any orders given. The responsibility and the running of this operation remains with you, Lieutenant James."

The following day I was informed that the meeting previously arranged for the full complement of both governments to attend for a briefing had been cancelled and suddenly the five of us found ourselves being shipped very quickly with a very strong detachment of MPs to an naval base somewhere on the east coast. Waiting for us was a fast-looking ship and no sooner had we boarded than the order to cast off was given and we were hustled down below.

Every form of comfort was ours for the asking. It was then that the captain came into view.

"I'm Captain Michael O'Leary," and he informed us that our stay with the ship would be approximately 36 hours and that we could move around the ship and enjoy the trip until called. Once again we were advised to get plenty of rest.

We were called at 0330 hrs, some 33 hours later. We had apparently made very good time. We assembled on deck. It was very dark and everyone was looking to port so we did the same. Only a few minutes later and with a slight hiss of escaping air, a submarine came to the surface. It must have been waiting for our arrival.

The captain of the ship appeared and said, "Good luck."

Our transfer to the sub went ahead without an order being given. Once below again, that hiss of air and we all knew we were on our way. It was then that Commodore Griegson appeared.

"So we meet again, gentlemen. I see you have yourselves an addition to your party. Your stay with us will be about two days and a night, so rest up and if you need anything just ask. I'll arrange for you to have a look around our home, but for now I suggest a good night's sleep."

The trip went very well, but all too quickly. The commodore requested our presence in his cabin and told us that we would be at our destination in six hours and he had arranged for our equipment to be available to do any checking we may like to do and would we please be ready to disembark by 0200 hrs.

0245 hrs, North Africa, mid July 1963 – About a mile from the coast, one of HM submarines, somewhere in the Mediterranean, very gently came to the surface in what could be described as a very calm sea. With hardly any noise, men started to appear from a hatch and in a very short time they had launched a large rubber dinghy. But they wasted no time. Once the task was completed, they simply disappeared back down the hatch. Once the dinghy was away from its side, and with some hissing of air, the sub very quickly slipped back down to periscope depth. No doubt someone was still keeping a eye on us.

The dinghy had a crew of five, all dressed entirely in black. It also had five passengers: Mac, my three team mates and myself. Danny was my number one, Knocker my number two and Timber my number three. We had been a team for over a year. On or off duty we got on very well together. Danny, Knocker and Timber have, on many occasions, proved to be the best in our kind of business and being their team leader, this is greatly appreciated. It makes my job a lot easier. We had now successfully completed several missions, similar to the one we were about to undertake.

We were trying to keep out of the way of our five chauffeurs, who were making very good progress towards the shore. Who could blame them? The sooner they shed their load, only when back on the sub would they fill safe again.

About 200 yards out from the shore the muffled motor was cut. Three of the crew moved without a sound and picked up Sterling automatics, one to the port side, one to the starboard side and one in the bow. They gave us the feeling that we were in the hands of experts and by the way they moved this was not the first time they had performed this task.

After a short time, the dinghy ran gently up the sandy beach and stopped. No one made a move until the lookout in the bow indicated that it was all clear to do so. With a nod and a whispered word of good luck from our friendly lookout, myself, Mac and the team slipped over the side and quickly made our way up the beach.

We hit the deck at the ridge and all five of us did a 360-degree check. I looked back for the dinghy but it had already disappeared. There was nothing for it but to push on. We had about six miles to go before digging in and camouflaging up, which had to be done well before sun up. It was a very dark night, just made for our kind of work, but we all found that the going was not very good and we had to keep stopping to check our bearings. All the same, we made very good time and were in position well before the sun was due to appear.

We had picked our spot well. We had dug in and camouflaged our position. The daytime sun should not be any trouble to us. We could see the lights of a nearby town, which must be Misratah, and there was a very busy road not more than a mile away. On checking our map, the landing must have been spot on, thanks to the navy. That was a great start for our next move.

Timber was doing a final 360-degree sweep and was studying a section on our left flank with great interest.

"Guv, you are not going to like this but there's a bloody great army camp over to our left."

"This is no time for your bloody silly jokes," said Knocker, at the same time having a look for himself. "Bloody hell, guv. He's right and it's a beehive!"

"Mac, take the rear. Danny, take the right," and with that I joined Timber and Knocker. How we had missed the camp on our arrival to our chosen spot I will never know. "Everyone stay in your present positions while I work out a new route for tonight."

It was then that Mac, in his slow southern drawl, said, "Guv, here's something else you are not going to like. We have company in the form of a five-man patrol heading this way."

"All of you keep watching your fronts and at the same time stay well hidden but be ready for anything. On no account are you to fire unless I do," and with that I joined Mac.

The hostile patrol was still heading our way, it must have been only about 50 yards away when they started to veer to the left towards the camp.

"Timber, they are coming your way. Keep an eye on them."

I slipped down into our cubbyhole and carried on with planning the route out of there. When I had completed this, I made sure that we all understood our new route. It was just a very simple thing we were to cross the road at a point one mile south of our intended crossing.

We once more settled down but remained in position and on watch. We had something to eat, mainly dried fruit and desert chicken, washed down with lukewarm water and then got as much rest as we could. It was now 0400 hrs so we had about two hours before sun up. We had to remain hidden for the rest of the day before making our next move. We all agreed it would be okay to do shifts of one hour on and three off in the daytime. We understood each other so well. We just rested, sleep was out of the question on a mission like this. The slightest noise and all five of us were wide awake.

The sun had been up about two hours when the tinkling of bells had all five of us checking the full 360 degrees. It was a herd of goats with two "bints" looking after them. They were very close but all five of us agreed they had not seen us. It was just then that the one in a red dress squatted down, leaving a wet patch before catching up with the herd. That okayed everything – no woman would do a thing like that if she thought she was being watched.

The rest of the day passed very slowly. All of us got restless and could not wait for it to get dark just to get moving again and at long last it was once more very black and time to get on the move. We uncovered our packs, checked our weapons and I checked our bearings. With one last look around to see that we had left nothing to give away our presence, I reminded them all to keep a look out for any patrols now that we knew they operated in the area.

So we made our way once more across the very unpleasant, stony sand to our designated target area, which was a large house about two miles away. We got to a very busy road. It must have been a popular town because the traffic was continuous and we had a hell of a job crossing. The new route had cost us many valuable minutes; we still had time in hand but any more delays like that and it would be tight getting to the target. We had made up some time in spite of the road traffic and the rough terrain.

We finally arrived and picked a spot about 150 yards from the target house. We had good cover and could see three sides of the house. Then we mapped out our exit routes; we always make two, but this time we decided to return the same way we had come because the only delay we had was the road. I had a look around and could not see any guards, only barbed wire on top of the walls. That was not going to be a problem for us as we had no intention of entering the compound. I passed the glasses to Danny and after all of us had made a sweep of the area and compound, we decided to stay put. So now it was just the case of waiting for the target to appear and as always it seemed like hours. But shortly after that, Danny whispered, "Skipper, three o'clock, bright lights coming over the hill."

It was not long before three cars with their headlights and spotlights blazing could be seen coming along the road at very high speed. As they entered the compound, the lights came on. The combination of the house lights and the compound lights made it just like a film set. Not only that, about 30 well-armed men appeared. These kind of surprises we did not like. Half of them made for the gate and the others ran in all directions, some of them even firing in the air. The cars came to a screeching stop inside the compound. It was so very easy to pick out the target, he was a very big man dressed in flowing white robes and headdress. He must have weighed about 25 stone and he was waving his arms about like a mad man. Somebody was getting a good roasting; something was not to his liking. He slowly got himself under control and made for the house. The escort and drivers, all in very great haste, got back into the cars and started to leave, once more with their lights blazing and at high speed.

We waited until they had disappeared back the way they had come. We gave it about 15 minutes to let our eyes get accustomed to the dark again and then started to have one more look around. Everyone had now gone back inside the house and most of the lights in and around the compound had gone out, only the house lights remained on.

Danny and I did another check of the house while Knocker and Timber kept watch on the flanks as we could not see the back of the house. Once again Mac was taking care of the rear and at the same time taking everything in and keeping out of the way. Those 30 armed men could not be accounted for. The area was checked once again by the lads. Their reply was "A-okay to proceed".

I closed my eyes for a few seconds to get them accustomed to the subdued lights that had remained on and I then started to look for the target, which had also gone inside the house. We had been told he always used the top right-hand room with a balcony. They had got that right for a change, for there he was, big, bright and beautiful, walking up and down the balcony, still fanning himself. I checked with the others just to make certain that everything was ready for a quick departure. Once again the reply was "A-okay".

I got myself in a good firing position and waited for the target to stop walking around or sit down. It seem like hours before a servant appeared with a tray and then he did both, he stopped and sat down right in front of the window. I could not help but wonder where all the guards had gone. What were they thinking of, letting him sit there? The set up could not have been any better. One last check with the lads and back to the job in hand. I now had the target in my sights. I slowly let the air out of my lungs, taking up the first pressure on the trigger and slowly squeezed.

The No. 4 Mk1 rifle recoiled into my shoulder and made its usual sharp crack as the bullet passed through my homemade flash guard. I saw the look of amazement on the target's face and the blood spreading over his white gown. I worked the bolt action for the second shot and seeing that the target was still sitting more or less upright, I gently squeezed the trigger once more. There was more blood, but this time he fell forwards out of sight.

The target was down. There was no other movement at first and then all hell broke loose. All the lights came on again and guards were running in every direction. It was time to get out of there.

I looked around. The others had heard the rifle and were already making preparations to move. One last look towards the target, just to make sure. He was down all right.

I said, "Let's get the hell out of here."

We had been going for about an hour and my number two, Knocker, was in the lead and I was next in line, checking the compass and keeping us on course. It's so easy to make a mistake on these black nights but Knocker had done very well because just in front was the mud hut we had stopped at going the other way. We had made good time and stopped to check our bearings.

Knocker turned to say something, when without any warning, a short burst of fire came from just in front of the hut. Knocker went down as if pole-axed.

We all returned a short burst of fire and could hear a low moaning coming from within the hut. I turned to Mac and said, "Look after Knocker."

I slipped out of my pack and at the same time indicated to Danny to take the right and for Timber to take the left. I took my knife and went very gingerly towards the sound of our unseen attackers. Inside the hut I found two dead and my knife helped the other one on his way to Mecca. Out of the hut I went to the right and I had only gone a few yards when I came face to face with a grinning Danny. We both went looking for Timber and kept coming across discarded equipment. Not long after that we saw Timber wiping his knife on the shirt of number five. His trail very clearly indicated that he had been heading for the new camp. The firing had already done the job for him and the camp was in a turmoil.

We headed back to Mac and Knocker, not knowing what to expect. We had no need to worry, Knocker was taking it easy on lookout while Mac had been busy getting our packs ready for a quick move. Apparently his backpack had taken the impact and it had only winded him.

"Lucky sod," I said and we all had a good laugh.

It was then that Knocker said, "Guv, two mobile patrols are heading our way."

I asked him if he was up to it.

"No sweat, guv, no sweat. Please may we get the hell out of here?"

We made a very fast exit from the mud hut, back tracked for about half a mile, stopped and did 360-degree sweep. We rested for five minutes and then turned south and still going very fast, headed for our RV with the navy. After about a mile we found a *wadi* going in the right direction. We rested and after another 360-degree check we could only see one patrol heading away from us. How lucky could one get? The *wadi* gave us very good cover and we made good time and we were able to follow it almost up to the road. The road was very quiet; no civilian vehicles, only stationary army vehicles spaced out with their headlights on making a ribbon of light. How could we cross?

It was Mac who had been scanning the area through the night glasses and said, "Guv, take a look at the third tanker from our left. I think he's sitting on a continuation of the *wadi*. Looks like water drain of some kind."

We all took a look and decided to have a go. The pipe was a bit tight but we made very good use of it. Someone up there was looking after us. The *wadi* now started to veer away from our RV. I did not like leaving our very friendly *wadi* but the time situation made the decision for me. We were still well behind on time and if we were late getting to our RV the sub commander would give us a good going over. They don't like being submerged in shallow water, but now back to it and we still had a bit to do and that firing must have woken up the everyone for miles. We had to be on our toes even more so from then on.

"Right, let's leg it and get to the beach. We have an appointment with the navy that we do not want to miss."

Now that we were close to reaching the RV, we were that bit more careful. It was Danny, who was following at number two, whispered, "Guv. On our right someone has just taken a drag on a fag."

As usual, on stopping we all went to a firing position. I was with Danny and this time we both noted the position of our smoking friend. After another check, we both decided that it was only one man, who must be a lookout for a patrol resting or laying in wait.

Time was getting short. I called up Knocker and explained what was needed. He just nodded and slipped away.

It was not that long after when he slid alongside me and said, "Just the one, guv. He was looking after a load of kit."

"Knocker, you frightened the life out of me."

He gave a big grin and said, "Sorry, guv."

That meant a patrol was out there and they must have been waiting for us. I sent Danny to the right and Timber to the left and told Mac to watch our rear. Knocker and I took centre; we moved very slowly, first the centre then the flanks. It was Danny who signalled first, slipping over to the centre and pointing them out to me. I called the team together and pointed out their targets.

"I'll look after anyone not accounted for. We shall have to come back for our kit."

It was all over in five minutes and there was Mac with a big grin on his face, saying, "Thanks, guv."

We made the RV with just a few minutes to spare. We checked our position was clear, signalled to our pick-up and took up position once again along the waterline. It was not long before the navy arrived. It was the same crew.

"Nice to see you again," said the navy crew. "Let's go home to mother."

They must have been watching us because there, about 50 yards ahead, the sub as silently as before showed itself. The dinghy gently ran up to the side and we were hustled below. It was then that we met our chauffeurs with big grins, handshakes and pats on the back all round. We were then shown to our quarters, given clean clothes and allowed to take a hot shower. We were then served our first hot meal for four days – the navy's steak and kidney pie and a good tot of Navy rum.

We were all getting stuck into the meal when Mac stood up and said, "Gentlemen, I would like to say it has been a pleasure and a privilege to have been in your company for the last few weeks, especially the last ten days. I thank you all."

"Oh, for Christ's sake, Mac, sit down and eat the food. It's too good to miss and make speeches," said Timber.

"Don't you guys ever take things serious?" Mac asked.

I was then called to the captain's cabin, who asked if I and my team had been made comfortable and was there anything else we needed.

I said, "Thanks to you and your crew for what you have done. You all made our job that much easier. But I think I had better make my report now."

Once this had been completed, I made my way back to our quarters.

About two hours later I was once more called to the captain's cabin, who must have been in radio contact with the powers that be. He told me that the team and I, with Mac, were to be taken to Gibraltar where we were to be stationed for some R and R and kitted out with civvies in readiness to go to the United States to meet our equivalents in the American Special Services. He said he could not enlighten us as to what lay ahead, but wished us all good. He then indicated that the officer standing close by would take care of us.

The young officer turned and said, "This way, gentlemen."

Mumbai Memories

As the musical tempo changed, so the invited guests for the passing out of the officer cadets at Sandhurst College in Camberley, Surrey, started to move for a better viewing position. I did the same as memories had started to flood back to my days of being just as proud of passing out in front of my parents as those on parade today.

It was then that a voice from the past, some 24 years before and one I had longed to hear again, very softly said, "That's one of your sons being presented with sword of honour."

Twenty-four years earlier, almost to the day and while in India, that same soft voice had captured my heart.

"Hello. I'm Mrs Aurora Philips of Philips Shipping. Since my husband's death I've been the new managing director and I would be very pleased to continue with our present arrangements. I also thank you for your very kind invitation to tonight's party."

"That's my pleasure, Mrs Philips. It's very nice to of you to attend."

I could not stop looking at her, she was stunning. We arranged to meet after the speeches. They seemed to go on for ever but she appeared out of the crowd and I suggested a walk around the extensive grounds, even though I was the host, but alas my secretary soon summoned me. I quickly made arrangements to meet her the next day at the

Peninsula Grand Hotel in Madhuradas Vasanji Road at ten o'clock for coffee.

She arrived looking like a princess and I knew I was in love with her. I suggested a drive to the coast and we arrived at Murud, which had a inlet with the very famous fort. After a short visit, we found a beach which gave us the solitude we sought.

We both became very passionate, kissing and fondling each other as if we knew that it was meant to be. It was then late in the afternoon and the wind started to get chilly so we headed for the Sandpiper Hotel for coffee and the use of the facilities.

On her return from the ladies room, Aurora said, "I hope you will not mind but I've booked a room for the night. Would you care to join me?"

My reply, which may have sounded somewhat over keen, was, "Yes, I would love to join you."

The night in question was unforgettable. All the built-up passion we had to give was truly a wonderful feeling of the love we held for each other. We must have slept for a short time and I slowly came to, reaching out for Aurora, only to find an empty space. I called but there was no reply. I looked but there was no sign of my lovely Aurora.

I quickly showered and dressed and went to the reception desk where I was told that "Madam" had left earlier by taxi.

As soon as I arrived at my office I put a call in to Philips Shipping and asked for Mrs Philips, only to be told that she was not available, her location was unknown and no further information was available. I felt as if my world had fallen apart and went home to think.

Three days later my secretary called at my home, saying she could not continue to put things off and needed me to return as a lot of the company's business required my attention.

No matter how I tried to locate my Aurora, even a private detective returned a negative report and several years later I was promoted and transferred to our London office in St James's Square. For company business, I joined several clubs, including the Naval and Military Club in St James's Square and also the Army and Navy Club in the same area, as well as several others. This was where business matters could be carried out in a more leisurely way.

It was at such a meeting that I met an old acquaintance from my army days who very kindly invited me to Sandhurst for the day. It would be the day that my Aurora returned to me with those very soft words: "That's one of your sons being presented with the sword of honour."

I turned and my daily prayer had at long last been answered because standing there, looking as beautiful as ever, was my dream, my Aurora. We embraced and exchanged a kiss on the cheek, but I held on to her, fearing to let go just in case I lost her again.

The music had stopped and we walked towards a group of young men. One of them stood out as he was holding the sword of honour and looking very smart in his uniform of the Indian Army. Another was dressed in a very expensive suit and looking just as smart.

The two young men turned, saw Aurora and said, "Mother, did you enjoy the parade?"

"Immensely," she replied. "I'm a very happy and proud mother of my two fine sons."

After a short pause she held the hands of her two sons, saying, "Now, I would like you to meet a very good friend of mine. Colonel, or if you like, Mr Ronald James."

The pause this time was a lot longer but Aurora continued by saying, "Who also happens to be your father."

The two boys and I looked first at Aurora and then we looked at each other as the announcement was surely an explosive one.

I was still reeling from Aurora's announcement, but looking at the two boys, I said, "Seeing that this is the time for surprises, and it may seem presumptuous to you young gentlemen, but I ask your permission for your mother's hand in marriage."

Once again it went very quiet, but the newly appointed officer, after first looking at his brother, stepped forward and saluted, saying, "Permission granted, sir. My brother and I would be very proud."

We all looked towards Aurora, who kept us waiting but then said, "I would be very pleased to marry you," and with that we all started to laugh and talk at the same time.

We were married on July 21st at a very pleasant little church in Murud and stayed at the Sandpiper Hotel and, well, that's where it all started.

Three "Ms" Plus One

It was a bright, sunny and warm Sunday at about two o'clock in the afternoon. I was heading towards home and had had just left the drill hall in South Wimbledon after attending my army cadet training. I felt on top of the world, all dressed up in my khaki uniform with my bright white sergeant's stripes for all to see.

My name is Leslie James. I'm six feet tall with light hair, almost blond, and with hazel eyes. At nearly 16, I have a reasonably well-built body that was due to our Dad putting my brother Ken and me and on a daily exercise routine of running and shadow boxing first thing each morning before we went on our paper rounds. Dad used to box in the Territorial Army and loved to show us his silver statue, cups and medals that he won as a flyweight. We think he had visions of both of us taking up boxing, sorry Dad.

I'm enjoying my walk towards home and as usual I'm dreaming of joining the real army and I try to imagine what it would really be like. I could see there was the large removal van outside number 125 and me being the inquisitive type, I walked over and said, "Hello, I'm Leslie. I live at number 141. Can I be of any help?"

That was my first meeting with the Brownings.

Mrs Browning was about 40, 5ft 10ins tall and her hair was long, black and very shiny with a slight curl. Her eyes were a very bright sparkling green and they seemed to be laughing along with you. Her body would have been the envy of any woman; the shape was just about perfect.

She was a very lovely lady, and in response to my offer of help, she said, "Thank you for your kind offer but the girls can manage. They are doing a great job and they know where everything has to go."

It was then that all three girls appeared. They were just like their Mum – all very good looking – and without stopping they called out, "Hello!" but carried on with the unloading, but not without a lot giggling and girly laughing coming from the van.

My next meeting with a member of the Browning family was about six weeks later. It was a Wednesday and my half day off from work. I was about to go to the library for my Dad to change his books and that's when I bumped into Marion, who was one of the twins and who just happened to be going to the library as well. We hit it off right from the start and she waited for me for the return trip.

On our way she asked me if I would show her some of the local country walks as she would love to observe as much of the local wildlife as she could.

I said, "You're in luck. As it so happens, it's my half day and I would love to take you to Cannon Hill Common where you might be lucky seeing a wild deer and a rabbit or two." So we made arrangements to meet up 30 minutes later.

Now Marion was about the same age as me, just under 16. She and her twin sister, Margaret, were the spitting image of their mother. Marion had very long dark brown hair and her eyes were big and dark blue and had the same twinkle as her mothers. Her body, just like her Mum's, was as near perfection as could be. I had a funny feeling about the walk, but nevertheless I did a quick change and was ready in 20 minutes as I just could not wait to get started.

As I walked up their, drive the door opened, she must have been looking out for me. She was certainly not dressed for walking. I said nothing because she looked just great.

At the common I said, "One of the best places would be over at the copse where the trees will hide us."

But she had other ideas, saying, "Let's sit here for a bit, we just might see a squirrel. It was a great spot and we would be completely surrounded by thick shrubbery. I could not have picked a better spot for what she had in mind because as soon as I sat down she pushed me down flat on my back and started to kiss me as if the end of the world was about to happen. I did not mind one little bit as I was hoping something like this would be on the cards and not only that, I was truly enjoying myself and even helped her out by responding.

Once she could see that I was game, she started with my shirt buttons, pulling my shirt off. The next thing, with a giggle, was her blouse, which came off revealing that she had no bra on. I was looking at two very firm white breasts and she lent over me brushing two very hard, red, cherry like nipples across my lips. I was in a state of high passion that I had never known before and I completely joined her in the pleasures we both obviously sought and found in each other.

She stood up and slowly started to remove the rest of her clothing, just standing there and looking down at me with a very big smile and then bending over and helping me with mine because I was memorised by what I was seeing and I felt as if I were paralysed. But with a little more effort on my part we found ourselves as nature had intended us to be – naked – and our remaining clothing had been discarded into two untidy piles of clothing. We clung to each other in the rich green grass for the next few minutes and then she started to run her hands over me but that was not what she wanted as she had already found my manhood, which was as hard as I had ever known it to be, and like a new toy she was being very gentle handling it. As she did so, we both moaned with pleasure.

She at once took the position of being on top, gently easing herself onto me, where she was able to help herself. Which she did with great gusto, working like a steam engine up and down, up and down, until she collapsed alongside me. Her eyes were shut but with a great big grin she said, "Thank you."

I was just lying they're looking at her spent, perspiring body glistening from the passion she had shown me. I could only feel my body trembling and I knew I wanted more. She must have realised what I wanted because she pulled me onto her, saying, "Yes please," and as I entered her, she gave that little moan once again and pulled me even closer.

This time it was me that was the steam engine, thrusting just that bit harder and deeper each time until Marion said, "No more!" But I just could not stop myself and my fully built-up passion spent itself within that tunnel of love.

This time we lay they're not only gasping for breath but with the realisation of what we had done and what consequences from our spent passion could be coming our way.

We slowly dressed and our walk back home was also a slow one and a very quiet one. When we reached number 125 we made arrangements that she would contact me in a week or two. I decided not to tell Mum or Dad, which in the end proved to be the right decision.

It was ten days later when there was a knock on the front door and Mum called me, saying, "Ron, it's Marion. She wants to talk to you." With that I grabbed my coat and we walked through the farm mint fields.

Once out of earshot of anyone, Marion told me, "All's well but the next time we must take precautions."

"Oh!" I said. "Is there going to be a next time?"

"You can bet on it," she replied with a great big grin and with that we found a soft bed of mint and the next time had arrived.

As it turned out, I did not see Marion or her sister Margaret for nearly three months. They had been shipped off to their uncle and aunt's, who lived near Brighton in Sussex, at a place called Peacehaven, so that Marjorie, their Mum and Mavis, their sister, could get on and decorate the house. But I did receive a postcard from Marion, which I decided to show Marjorie. So that evening I called at number 125. The door was only half opened by Marjorie, who only had a loose-fitting bathrobe on.

I said, "If your busy I can come back some other time."

"Hello, Leslie. It's so nice to see you. Mavis has gone to the late show at the cinema, but please come in."

I explained why I had called, showing her the card.

"Oh! That is nice of you. Here, let's sits down so that I can read what Marion has to say."

We sat on the Chinese rug in front of the fireplace as everything had dust covers on it because the decorating had started. As we sat down, I could not help but noticing that the bathrobe had fallen open revealing those long, lovely legs leading up to that very desirable and shapely body and making the shiny pubic hair stand out. Marjorie looked up from reading the card and I could see that her eyes were bright and shining a lot brighter than normal. They kind of mesmerised me and she must have seen this in me because she took both my hands and placed them on her breasts. I could feel the firm red nipples and she immediately started to tremble and gave that low moan, just like Marion had. I freed one of my hands and pulled the cord on her bathrobe, which then slowly slipped from her shoulders to the floor, completely revealing her body with all its beauty to its fullest possible advantage.

It was my first time I had seen an older female body so completely naked and it was then that I felt the need to hold one. The one I was looking at was just so perfect and as I reached out I felt a warm sensation running through me. As I held on to Marjorie I could feel my body getting that much warmer and I held on tightly, not wanting to let go,

Her response was so unexpected; she kissed me fully on the lips and started very hastily to take my cloths off. The kissing went on but this time I could feel her tongue playing with my throbbing manhood, sending my blood pressure so high that I to started to moan. We lay there, both knowing that we wanted each other and while laying there, I fondled and kissed her all over, my tongue and lips playing with the hard red nipples. After exploring each other until we knew the time was right, she pulled me on top of her, crossing her legs behind me so there was no going back, but I had no intention or thoughts of that kind. I was throbbing down below and she was trembling. As I entered her she gave a long sigh and after about ten minutes I started to slow down but in a low whisper she said, "Not now, my lover, not now."

Shortly after that we climaxed as one and we both lay there breathing very heavily but also very contented and happy. I know I was.

It must have been some time before she rolled over, kissed me and said, "That was very nice," and somehow we managed to find the energy to satisfy each other again and again. Laying down once more getting our breath back, we just held hands.

It was on our way to the bathroom, with the intention of taking a shower together, that open door to her bedroom was too much for both of us and we stumbled into the room with that inviting bed and just started all over again. After that we took separate showers and once dressed, it was peck on the cheek at the door.

"Thank you for showing me the card," she said.

I only had a few yards to walk to home but it did give me time to think. The experience was out of this world and the pleasure was mind-bending for a nearly 16-year-old. Something I would remember for a very, very long time.

It was about six weeks later when Marjorie told me that her husband, Ray, was coming home on leave and we had better stop our meetings for the time being. The very next day, on my way home from the shop for lunch, that I spotted this Royal Navy chap struggling with two very large suitcases.

Being on the shop bike, which had a carrier attachment on the front, I said, "Would you like a hand with those? They look very heavy."

"That's very good of you," he replied.

It was only then that I realised who he was.

I said, "Does your name happen to be Browning?"

"That's right," he replied. "How do you know that?"

"I've been a friend of your family since they moved into number 125."

Now that I knew who I was speaking to, I had a second look at him. He was a handsome chap; a great catch for any woman. He was just over 6ft with hair going grey at the temples, that's about all I could see because his hat and uniform covered the rest and with all that gold braid, I knew I would have to call him sir next time we met.

We arrived at number 125. Mavis and Marjorie must have seen us coming because they both came running towards us. They made such a fuss of him, which I could understand, so I just left the cases on the doorstep and carried on home.

Just about a week later, I bumped into Mavis, the eldest of the girls, and I asked how her dad was getting on.

"He's doing very well, in spite of his wounds. Mum is fussing over him all the time. Thank you for helping him with those suitcases, he must have been struggling with them and they weighed a ton when I tried to lift them."

Mavis then told me that he had received his injuries whilst on patrol in the China Sea and was on sick leave awaiting orders for his next posting.

As we got closer to number 125, I said, "Tell the captain I wish him well."

"Oh! Don't call him captain, his name is Ray." Mavis went on to say, "Les, would you be a dear and take me out on Sunday? You see, I would love to give Mum and Dad some time to be on their own."

She's asking me out, I thought. I'd been trying to pluck up the courage to ask her out myself. Now Mavis was of the same build as her parents, she was 5ft 10ins tall, with long black hair just like her mum. Her eyes were a pale green and always had that twinkle that made you notice them and her body was also just like her mum's – perfection at its best.

"You're in luck," I said. "I have some time owing to me and yes, I would love to take you out."

So arrangements were made to go to Southend by Surrey Motor Coaches. The boarding point was outside the pub The Grapes in the High Street and on our arrival at ten o'clock, alongside Southend's Kursaal, the driver, with a voice like a foghorn, shouted out, "We leave at six o'clock! Sorry but we cannot wait, so please be on time!"

We headed for one of the many cafés had breakfast and then purchased sandwiches and drinks, along with a windbreak as the sun might have been out but there was a slight wind blowing.

We found a spot to our liking for a bit of sunbathing, fixed up the windbreak, laid out the towels and got ready for some serious sunbathing. Mavis had this very tiny and skimpy bikini on, which she must have travelled down in. She looked so good.

As she lay down, she rolled over onto her tummy, saying, "Would you please rub some oil on my back? You'll have to undo my bra strap. I don't want strap marks."

That was the start of things and it was only a minute or two later when she rolled over and gave me a very nice kiss and at the same time showing me those two lovely, large and perfectly formed boobs. She had a look around and being satisfied, wriggled out of her bikini knickers and said, "That's better," giving me a big smile.

I made to put my arms around her but she pushed me away, saying, "Not now, lover boy, later."

I could not stop looking at her because she like her sisters and her mother, she was just perfect. I just lay there waiting for later to arrive and it was then that she opened her eyes and said, "Coward. Get your pants off."

I had a quick look around and then slipped them off, but I had to lie on my tummy straight away because I had a very large erection.

She had been watching and said, "My, my. You are a big boy, and in a hurry by the look of things." Then she closed her eyes, but she had a very big smile on her face.

It must have been about two o'clock when we both realised that it was very quiet out there. We both sat up, and found that the beach was almost deserted and it was then "later" arrived.

She was just as marvellous in her demands of me as the rest of her family and I'm pleased to say that I met her demands. We were also able to amaze each other in so many other ways and also the response was very pleasing for both of us and I once again found the enjoyment and the experience mind-bending.

We made our way back to the same café, had our refreshments and joined the coach for the journey back home. However, this time we managed to get the back seat and all the way home she gently rubbed my legs, knowing full well that I had this great erection.

We arrived at number 125 to find the place empty and with that she said, "I think we just have time to say goodnight in a bit more comfort."

Once again we surprised each other and I went home very happy. It had been a great day.

Now that Ray (Mr Browning) was at number 125, I had very wisely cut down my visits, which I think was appreciated by all, so when I heard Mum at the front door saying, "Please come in, Ray," I had my ears wagging.

I heard him say, "I've come to ask you to a party on Saturday week as I've received my promotion and my new posting to a training shore ship in Scotland. It's at a place called Scapa Flow, just south of Kirkwall, and the bonus is that I can take my family with me."

I went down the stairs as I had heard it all and I was on my way to the Kingston Empire to see the Crazy Gang.

"Hi, Ray. Can I come to the party too?" I asked.

"You will be more than welcome," he replied.

With that I said, "I'm off now, Mum, and congratulations, Admiral."

Mum said, "Don't you be so cheeky." But we all had good laugh.

On my return home from the theatre, I found Mavis sitting in the lounge waiting for me.

"Feel like taking me to the cinema, Les, my treat? There's a good film on and I don't like walking home alone at night."

"Give me a few minuets and I'll be with you."

It was a good film – Clark Gable and Vivien Leigh in *Gone with the Wind*. It was a long film and as soon as the end showed, we made a dash for the bus stop, only to find we had been beaten to it by so many others and so we decided to walk. It turned out to be the wrong thing to do because it started to rain very hard and we got soaked. When we arrived at number 125, Marjorie, her mum, could be seen waiting so it was a peck on the cheek from Mavis and a quick "Be seeing you".

I continued my short walk to number 141 and Mum took one look at me and said, "I'll run you a bath and warm your pyjamas. Leave your wet things and I'll see to them in the morning."

I said, "Thanks, Mum," and went off for a bath and then to bed.

In the morning I had a quick breakfast, just a piece of toast, to avoid any questions about the night before and went to work serving in the shop. Once again I gave the customers plenty of cheek, which helped the day go by very quickly. I was hoping for a good night with Mavis and I knew she was up for it.

As it turned out, Ray and the twins had gone to Scotland to look over his new posting and their new quarters. Marjorie had gone to visit some friends to tell them the news and so we had the house to ourselves, which proved to be one more night to remember as once again, completely naked, we surpassed each other's demands.

The night was going well, that was until Mavis started to cry, saying she did not want to go to Scotland because she loved the times we spent together. She then said that she loved me. Well, I'd had no thoughts along those lines and I was now in a state of shock. I very quickly got dressed and I'm pleased to say so did Mavis. We both went downstairs and sat on the settee and turned the TV on. As we did so, we both sat bolt upright as we could heard the key turn in the front door. Her Mum had come home early,

"Hello, you two. Had a good night?" she asked.

We both replied with great big grins, almost to the point of giving the game away. They both started to talk about how the others were getting on in Scotland and about family things and how they were looking forward to joining them. I looked over at Mavis, but she did not look my way and so I took the opportunity to make my excuses and leave, saying, "Hope you don't mind, I do have a big day tomorrow, which means an early night." Not only that, but with all the previous excitement that had taken place, I was truly ready for my bed.

Time had passed so quickly since the Brownings moved into number 125 and suddenly I was 17 and in five months and I could apply to join the army. That evening I went along to the recruiting centre to make inquires.

The sergeant, an old soldier with a lot of campaign ribbons on show, had talk with me, saying, "Your education and your cadet record should give you a good start," and then he gave me a form for both my parents to sign before he could consider my application.

On the way home I was doing some thinking about what lay ahead of me now that I had started the ball rolling for me to join the army. I had to pass number 125 going towards home and I looked over and just as I had hoped, the door opened and Marjorie gave a wave and beckoned me in, saying, "Could you please help me?"

It was not help she needed, it was me, and she really went to town and once again took control. Mind you, I wanted her just as much and that's why I had looked over towards number 125. The next hour once again turned into a night to remember because she was very demanding and it was not until we both lay there spent and breathing very deeply that she said, "Thank you. You always make me happy."

The next morning I showed Mum and Dad the form and they both looked at each other. Dad was the first to speak.

"Have you given it some thought, son?"

"Yes, Dad. I would like to join," I replied.

He signed, looking over at Mum.

She said, "I will have to think about it. Leave the form on the dresser."

I had a hard time with Mum but my persistence paid off in the end and a week later I presented the form to the recruiting sergeant, who, with a big smile, said, "I will mark it up, just as I said I would," and with that he shook my hand, saying, "You should hear from us in ten days."

While all this was going on, the Brownings had had their party, the twins and Mavis accompanied Ray and once again left for Scotland. Mavis had said no more about not wanting to go and all that about loving me, so with one big sigh of relief, I said to myself, goodbye Mavis.

During the next three days, Mum made several remarks that my spending a lot of time at number 125 had been noted. I did not make a reply but it was three days I will remember for a very long time, especially Sunday when we were at it all day and late into the evening and because the next day Marjorie would leave for Scotland. I did not see any of the Brownings again for a very long time.

My letter from His Majesty's government arrived two weeks later with instructions on how, where and why I was to report to the recruitment centre in Croydon for a medical and enlistment – if I passed the medical. I passed A1 without any problems and after having to swear to serve King and country for the next seven years, with five as a reservist, I was told to await instructions, which would take about ten to fourteen days.

Mine took three long weeks to arrive; I thought they had forgotten me. I was to report to the RTO at Kings Cross Station in London in two weeks' time at 1300 hrs on 21st July to travel to Northern Ireland to join the 28th Training Battalion for NCOs and officer training. I started to get excited and apprehensive at the same time but the time soon passed and I found myself saying goodbye to a crying Mum, with Dad saying, "Let me come with you as far as London."

Somehow I managed to start my new adventure alone and I arrived at Kings Cross Station well before the stated time. The RTO was a very large sergeant, a member of the Military Police, sitting behind a table with an army blanket over it.

"Good morning, sergeant. I have instructions to report to you by 1300 hrs."

He looked over my shoulder at one of the station clocks, saying, "Let's have a look at your papers," and once checked, he said, "Leave your gear here and go for a walk, but be back in one hour."

I had never been to this part of London before so I bought a sandwich and a drink, found a seat opposite number one platform and had a look at London. That's when a very tall, good-looking blonde said in a low, pleasant but husky voice, "When you have finished your sandwich, do you feel like having some fun?"

Before I could make any reply, two burly bobbies appeared and one of them said, "Is this person bothering you, sir?"

It was then that I realised the blonde was one of London's famous ladies of the night doing a bit of overtime.

"No, officer, the young lady was just asking if I would mind sharing my seat."

Once the bobbies were out of sight, she stood up and with a big smile said, "I owe you one. You are a toff," and promptly disappeared.

On my return, the RTO sergeant said, "You have a companion for the trip," and introduced me to a Harry Hunt.

Now Harry and I got on well from the start and it appeared that he was at the Croydon Centre on the same day as me. Our journey to Stranraer on Loch Ryan in Scotland was a pleasant one. The next morning we were expecting to be sailing for Northern Ireland but the ferry was cancelled due to bad weather and the army found us lodgings for the night. Mine was a very old terraced house with a dirty card with "B&B" on it.

On arrival, I was told by this rather scruffy old lady that I would have to share a bed. I told her no way would I be doing that. The landlady did not say anything and just walked away mumbling in a broad Scottish dialect. I had just brushed my teeth and was about to get into bed when the door burst open and standing there was this big, fat, dirty looking blonde, who after staring at me, said in a loud voice, "So you don't mind sleeping in my bed but you don't want to share it with me? Well, I've got news for you, my lovely boy, move over because I don't mind sharing with you and in the morning you'll be thanking me."

I must say, it was a night I shall not forget for a long time and I did think of thanking her. On top of that we did not sail for three days and the nights got better and better, but and in the end I was very pleased to leave for Ireland, just for the rest.

We set sail from Stranraer, the sea conditions having slightly changed for the better, but even so it was still a very rough sea and we did see a lot of Paddy's lighthouse. First it was the rocks below and the next we were looking over the top and how we managed not to be seasick, God only knew.

On our arrival to Northern Ireland at Port Larne, we were met by a very tall and very smart Irish Guards sergeant, who appeared to be disappointed that there were only 20 of us, but even so he soon had us seated on a coach which was painted in dark green and black camouflage markings, but the seating was comfortable.

Our arrival at the barracks made quiet a stir. Apparently we were to be an experimental group and once we all got settled in to what was to be our new home for the next six months and got to know each other, things started to happen. First was kit issue and a haircut, whether you needed one or not and then we were marched to the dining hall for our first taste of army cooking. It turned out to be very good, but not like Mum's.

My allotted bunk mate was a chap from Devon. His age and build were the same as mine and he had head of blonde hair so he became Blondie. He took the top bunk, leaving me the lower one. Harry unfortunately got lumbered with a chap from the East End of London by the name of Ray. We had plenty of space in this billet as there were only 20 of us. We had 3ft of space from the end of the hut and 5ft in between bunks.

The training was hard and there was a lot of it and it did not stop for six weeks. It was then that Ray from the next bunk told Harry, Blondie and I that he was thinking of doing a runner. He was picked up the next day trying to board a ferry without a pass and landed up in the camp cooler. Two days later he legged it from the cooler and this time made it back to Blighty and to his part of London. Harry had a letter from him a week later saying he had had enough of army life and was making a living in London.

Our first pass out had arrived and Blondie and I made our way to Belfast to do a bit of shopping. We had been along Donegal Street and into Victoria Street and as we were crossing the road outside the cinema, a young girl of about 19 and very heavily pregnant, started shouting and pointing at Blondie, saying, "That's the father of my child! That's him!"

The policeman controlling the crossing said, "I think you had better come with me, my lads."

The girl, her mother and father, Blondie and I, all landed up in the police station where Blondie and I were shown into one room and the girl and her family into another.

It was some two hours later that the police sergeant started asking us questions when I said that we had only been in Ireland for eight weeks and Blondie could not be the father as the girl had implied. He left us and five minutes later the girl and her father appeared.

You could see the girl was very scared and you could also see she had been crying a great deal. Her father was a big chap and said in a very deep Irish brogue, "Go on, say you're sorry to the young man."

A very faint voice said "Sorry."

The sergeant said, "You might as well go now, my lads."

Once again, Blondie said, "Sergeant, we are out on pass and our curfew was ten o'clock. Would you please phone the camp?"

He thought for a moment and then said, "Wait there."

The police car took us to the camp and the police sergeant told the guard commander what the situation was, but we still ended up in the cooler for the night.

The next morning we told our story to the commanding officer, who just burst out laughing, saying, "Dismissed.

And, Sergeant Major, see that they get the rest of the day off."

On our next weekend pass we decided to spend it in the local area of Hollywood, just north of Belfast. That's how we met Vi and Molly, but alas it was too late all we could say was, "If you're around next weekend, we will meet you at the Riverside Café."

Now Blondie and I kept passing comments as to which one was going with who and pulling each other's leg over the two girls. In the end I got to go with Vi, who was a bit plumper than Molly but in the end she turned out to be a real goer and she always wanted more. But I pleased her because with all that training I was fitter than ever and was able to keep up with her demands. Boy, was that a night. Even if we had to be back in camp by ten o'clock, it was a very active and full night and my bed was a welcome sight. I don't think Blondie even got undressed and I wondered what he had been getting up to.

The big day came when our six long months of training had been completed and we were fully trained and ready to go to our regiments. Both Blondie and I had been promoted twice during the six months and we were both now corporals.

The passing-out parade was just one great big spectacular show and how proud we were to be taking part. The word had gone round that orders had been posted and we all made a rush to read them. Blondie was homeward bound to Devon and the Devonshire Regiment and was to go to the East Surrey Regiment in Canterbury as an instructor.

Three weeks later and with Rob in tow, we made it to Waterloo Station and whilst saying our goodbyes, who should walk up to us but Ray, looking very unkempt but still in his uniform.

He said, "Nice to see you soldier boys again, but I can't stop, the Red Caps are all over the place," and with that he just disappeared into the crowd. Well, I never saw Blondie or Rob again. Well, that's life for you.

We all had two weeks leave before reporting to our respective units and I could not wait to see Mum and Dad so it was down into the underground I went, heading for Morden Station and a taxi to number 141.

When I got home, I just rested for the rest of the day and let Mum make a fuss over me. Dad just wanted to know what this and that was like and how did everything work, so I said, "How about us all going to the pub and getting some fish and chips, my treat?" And that was agreeable to all.

The next morning was Sunday and I bumped into Pat from next door just as her parents were going to church. It was her mother who said, "Stay and talk to Pat," and with that off they went leaving us to talk.

Pat's first words were, "Let's go upstairs and carry on where we left off."

She had a good memory and she had not forgotten anything. It was a really steamy morning and nearly two hours later I returned home, avoiding Mum because I was shattered and the best place for me was my bedroom and I needed my rest after being with Pat.

My leave seamed to go very quickly but in a way I was pleased to be going back to the army and now with the gentle sway of the train heading for Canterbury as per my orders, I had time to think about what may lay ahead for me.

On my arrival I asked the station master if I could use his phone to ring the camp.

"Yes," he said as he walked towards the train guard. "You'll find it in the office."

It was the guard room sergeant that answered and when I explained who I was and could he arrange transport for me, he just said, "What do you think this, a taxi office?" and slammed the phone down.

I phoned again and this time I got the operator and asked for the duty officer. On explaining who I was and what had taken place, he said that I was expected and that transport would be with me shortly.

The transport arrived in the form of a very dirty Austin PU and the driver was just as bad. He was a complete mess and taking one look at me, he said, "Blimey, mate, where have you come from, Buckingham Palace?"

"I'm Corporal James and as from now you will address me as Corporal. Now take me to the orderly room."

No more was said, and on reporting to the orderly room I was told that I was to report on orders at 1500 hrs to see the commanding officer, which gave me time to have a shower and shave and smarten myself up.

Standing outside the orderly room I could not help but notice how badly run down the whole camp looked. On the dot I was marched in and I saluted, stating my name, rank and number, saying, "Reporting as ordered, sir," and that's how I got to meet the CO and the adjutant. But what I did not know was that they were as new to the camp as I was as the previous CO had been retired for medical reasons and that was the reason for the camp's run-down condition.

The commanding officer was a Lieutenant Colonel Watson, who just sat there looking at me and then towards the adjutant, a Captain Farmer. Both were from the Royal Engineers. He then looked back to me for maybe just over a minute, and as if he had just come out of a trance, he stood up, saying, "I'm very sorry about my manners. I think you are just what I was hoping for," and at the same time looking at the adjutant and asking, "What do you think, John?"

"I think you could be right there, sir."

The CO was now sitting on the front of his desk and told me why they had been posted there and that they were going to be needing a great deal of help to bring the camp back to a proper training establishment.

"So, Corporal James, you are to be my first shot at cleaning up and I would suggest you make a point of reading part-one orders tonight and see me at 1400 hrs tomorrow properly dressed."

I thanked him, saying I would very much like to help out and that I would not let him down. At that point they both shook hands with me and all three of us had great big smiles.

That evening I felt like a good meal so I made my way to the town and found a very smart hotel. The place was packed but I managed to get the last table. While waiting for my meal and enjoying a glass of red wine, the waiter asked if I would mind sharing my table, seeing that they were so busy.

I had not given any thought to who might be joining me but on his return, a very pleasant voice said, "This is so kind of you to let me share your table," and that's how I met Alexis, who was standing with her back to the well-lit foyer, which showed off her very pleasant figure. She was about 5ft 8ins tall with flowing black hair, but it was her eyes that seemed to sparkle and they were a bright green and stood out against her dark, tan skin.

The waiter took her coat and as she sat down. I ordered another bottle of wine, saying, "I hope you will join me in a glass or two."

"That's very kind of you," she replied and from then on we got on very well. We talked and talked; on my part I told her this was my first day in Canterbury and she told me that she had a small dress shop in the town and had felt like a meal out. We reached the last of the wine and I asked her if she would like to have a nightcap in the bar before saying goodnight.

That's when she said, "Not here. Why don't you walk me home and if you care to, we could have coffee at my place."

"That's okay by me," and with that, Alexis tucked her arm into mine as if she had know me for a long time.

Alexis's apartment was above her shop and it was very luxurious. We had the coffee and that's when she told me a little more about herself and her home town in Southern Italy, a place called Calabria, just south of Catauzaro on the east coast.

I was thinking that it was time to say goodnight when Alexis said, "Would you like to stay a bit longer?"

I explained that I had a big day tomorrow and really should get back to camp.

"Just stay a bit longer and I will take you back to camp in my car."

I could not say no to such a lovely lady, especially one I had started to have feelings for. We both knew what was expected of us and I realised that Alexis's needs were just as great as mine, but then my needs soon came to show as we both fulfilled each others pleasures. After having our showers, we made arrangements to see each other again and with that we dressed and went out to the car.

At the camp gates I lent over and kissed Alexis, who responded and said, "Don't leave it too long."

The sentry did not even look up from reading his book, which was just one more point to register for later. Outside the orderly room I could see part-one orders had been posted. In the first part I had been promoted to sergeant and in the next paragraph I had been promoted again, only this time to WO1 so I was now a sergeant major. It took some time for it to sink in but I was a very, very happy ex-corporal.

First thing next morning I handed my uniforms to the tailor, saying, "I would like one as soon as possible so that I can present myself to the CO properly dressed.

He said, "If you would care to take a seat, Sergeant Major, I will do one straight away."

I thanked him for his help and then took a walk around the camp, this time just making mental notes of what would be needed after my next meeting with the CO.

The meeting went very well. I was simply told that the camp needed to be shaken up and it would be my job to see that it was and that if I needed anything to just ask. So I did. I asked that the Military Police be requested to take over the security of the camp for one month. This was arranged and they arrived mid afternoon.

As soon as they arrived I had my own meeting with their sergeants in my quarters, explained the situation and we agreed on a plan that no one was to leave the camp unless the new MP guardroom sergeant was satisfied. But first of all it was "get your own back" time and I made my way to the guardroom where I told the sentry to stand the guard to.

He just spluttered, "Sorry, but I don't know how."

I walked over to the guardroom and told the sergeant to have the guard stand to. He just said, "What in bloody hell for?"

With that I called the MP sergeant over, saying, "That's it, take over and make the whole guard your first occupants. I'll be back shortly."

Realising that I had let my personal feelings get the better of me, I went back to my quarters to cool down. After about 20 minutes, I returned to the guardroom and this time told the sergeant that he would be on CO's orders the next day, on charge for neglect of duty in that he had not carried out his duties as laid down in his orders and for being in a state of undress while on duty. With that, he hit the MP sergeant in an attempt to get at me and it took three MPs to get him back into the cells. Then he was informed that the added charge of assault would be added. With that, the MP sergeant and I left him showing off his very bad temper by destroying the contents of the cell.

I spent the evening once again at Alexis's flat, where I had hoped to try and put the day's events behind me, but Alexis could see that I was still very tense and that something was playing on my mind.

After I'd told her of the day's events, she said, "Come on, I know what will ease both our problems," and with that she took my hand and led me to the bedroom where once again we seemed to enjoy trying to out do each other in our passions and I did, for a while, forget all my problems.

It was a full six months later; the MPs had long since gone and the camp was once more running to the satisfaction of the colonel. That's when I was summoned to his office and told that he had made a recommendation on my behalf and I had been accepted to attend the academy at Sandhurst for officer training.

That Friday night I had a very pleasant surprise for Alexis, who had booked a room for two nights at the Casa Hotel in Camberley so that both of us could have close look at the college. We had a good view of those very famous steps where the horse runs up to enter the grand hall.

It was a while later, when we were walking along the shops in Park Road when Alexis stopped and showed an interest in two adjoining shops and started to knock on the window to attract the attention of the two men who just happened to be there.

"Hello. I'm very sorry to trouble you, but are these two shops for sale?" she said.

It was the older one of the two who said, "Please come in."

In less than an hour it now appeared that Alexis had agreed to finalise the terms and would be the new owner of two prestigious double-fronted shops in a busy shopping street. Once the paperwork has been completed I was completely surprised as even I could work it out that those two shops must have cost a bomb.

That's when Alexis held my arm very tightly and said, "And now you know that I'm a very wealthy lady and in any case, I have been thinking of expanding the business and seeing that you will be here at Sandhurst for a year or more, I had no intention of letting you out of my sight because I love you very much."

That was the night I proposed to Alexis and we made plans to get married in a year's time.

That year passed very quickly and I'm now Second Lieutenant James and in a week's time I shall be getting married to my lovely Alexis.

Foreign Legion

My name is Leslie James and I live with Mum and Dad in a two-up, two-down in Sutton, Surrey. At Dad's insistence, I do exercise twice daily and I'm a well-built boy of 14 years, standing 5ft 10ins with a fine head of blond hair showing off my blue eyes. I leave school in three weeks with very little prospect of a job to help Mum and Dad with some income.

Mum and Dad are far from rich at the moment and they were having harsh words because Dad wanted to go for drink and Mum was not happy and was telling him that if he went for a drink, how could he expect her to keep food on the table? I felt so sorry for him as he was finding it very hard in those days to find work and could only get the occasional low-paid gardening work.

The next day I had gone farther afield than usual and found myself in Sutton high street shopping centre looking for a way of earning a bit of cash to give Mum. That's when I saw the poster outside the library saying "The French Foreign Legion needs you! Join here today".

It was a very impressive poster showing a very smart young man with a great big smile and wearing a very smart-looking uniform and a round shaped hat. I found out later that they call the hat a "Kepi". He was standing with a background of clear blue skies and with a very sunny outlook of rolling hills of sand with palm trees dotted around an oasis. I stood looking at that poster for a very long time, thinking it would be one less mouth for Mum to feed and Dad might get his drink.

On entering the building, a much older man than the one in the poster, but still just as smart, said with a very strong accent, "Good morning to you, my young sir. And what can I do for you?"

"I would like to join your army please, sir." I managed to splutter out. "But I would like to go home to say my goodbyes to my mum and dad before I do join, sir."

Now he was a very understanding sergeant and said, "Why not go and say your goodbyes and come back tomorrow."

The very next morning I said to Mum, "Would it be okay if I joined the army?" Not saying which army.

"Don't be silly. You're not old enough."

Dad piped up, "He could go as drummer boy." Now he was thinking of the English Army. Mum joined in in what she thought was a joke.

She was laughing but at the same time saying, "If you want to be a drummer boy, that's good, but don't forget to write home once in a while."

The next morning after a breakfast of one piece of toast with a scraping of margarine, I went back to have another look at the poster, having made my mind up.

To the surprise of the old sergeant, I once more said, "I would like to join your army please, sir."

After a lot of questions from the sergeant, I was shown into an office with an even older-looking man in a very smart uniform, which I took to be an officer's uniform. He too asked a lot of the same questions as the sergeant; mainly he kept on asking how old I was. I think he was trying to catch me out but I had already worked it out and in the end, one last time he said, "How old are you?"

But having the new birthday date firmly fixed in my head and as from that day I had a new birthday, which made me sixteen and three months.

The officer, looking over at the sergeant with a slight shake of his head said, "Very well, go with the sergeant and he will take care of you. Is there anything you need as I see you have brought very little with you?"

With tongue in check I replied, "I could do with something to eat and drink please, sir."

"Sergeant, see that he gets something to eat and drink."

With that, the sergeant said, "Follow me."

I spent two very nice days with the sergeant and his family and in that time they fed me gave me some new clothes and made a lot of fuss over me as if I were their own son. He also suggested that I write to my mother and father, which I did and he said he would see that it was posted.

I had been very well cared for and now the journey into the unknown would start, first by car and then by ferry from Dover and for the first time in my life I was standing on foreign soil. I was told it was Calais in France and there I was handed over to another smart sergeant. Both sergeants had a very long talk and kept looking my way, making me feel very uncomfortable.

My sergeant walked over shook my hand, saying, "You take care," and with that he held out his hand. While we shook hands he said again, "You take care."

As he walked away, I said, "Don't forget to post my letter, sergeant," and once again his words of "you take care" followed me.

Along with the new sergeant we approached a group of three, one of them being the very image I had seen on the poster, that smiling soldier from the Foreign Legion. The other two were in a sorry state; they both looked very tired and they must have been travelling a long time. One of them was very dirty and he was also in handcuffs, which did not help his appearance. I kept looking their way and started to wonder what lay ahead for me, but it was too late now. I was finding that I missed my dear mum and dad and I was feeling a bit homesick. I hoped they'd get my letter.

We arrived in Algiers after a long, hot, very bad and most uncomfortable boat ride. Then there was a journey by train to a place were all I could see was sand, no station as such, just sand. The train had stopped in the middle of nowhere. There were about ten of us that got off and we all stood there watching that old train puffing its away down the track that seemed to have no end.

We all started to follow our well-dressed "legionnaire" for what turned out to be a very long walk. It must have been six miles with the sun at twelve o'clock and the sand seemed to make it feel like you took one step forward and two back and were getting nowhere. Our travelling companion with the handcuffs was having a bad time of it so I gave him a helping hand and did my best to help him along. He just grunted and gave me a funny look, which made me shudder. After a spell we could see a long white wall with a very large black gate in the centre with the French flag flying in the gentle wind. This must be the training camp I had been told about and it was to be our home from that day on. As we passed through those black menacing gates I started to have mixed feelings again, but at the same time I was curious and excited to see more.

On our arrival most of the party disappeared leaving just the three of us standing in a very large courtyard. The first thing was the removal of the handcuffs by one very smart soldier from one of my travelling colleges and much to my surprise, the legionnaire soldier gave the handcuffs back to the man without a word being spoken by either of them. We were then taken to an office block and told to wait.

While standing there I had a good look around. I could not see a lot of movement and my fair-haired companion said in bad English, "They are at rest until it cools down."

At that moment I once again thought of the sergeant's words of "you take care". I wondered if he had posted my letter. It had only been a short one:

Dear Mum and Dad

Thank you for letting me join the army. I've been very well cared for, the food is very good and I have been issued with a complete new set of clothing. So you see, Mum, you have no need to worry and seeing that you have not got to feed me, maybe Dad can have that drink.

I will write again once I get an address for you.

Your loving son, Les.

At that moment the office door opened and a tall man in a very smart uniform, which told us he was a first sergeant.

He then said in three different languages, "Stand in a line."

Seeing as there are only three of us that was no problem. The first sergeant walked up and down three or four times not saying a word and then he spoke in German to the one who had at one time had been in handcuffs. I knew it was German as I had heard it before but did not understand what was being said. My travelling companion never said a word, just spat in the first sergeant's face. He was immediately taken away towards the guardroom but was still not saying a word. My remaining companion and I were shown a billet for the night and that's when we exchanged names and why we had joined.

I found out he was from Sweden, his name was Adam and he was on the run from a girl who had become pregnant and the girl's father was gunning for him. He had joined more or less the same time as me and from that day on we became firm friends and helped each other out in our army training and learning French and Arabic. Our training was hard and by the time the day was done and our kit was ready for the next day, we could only think of one thing and that was going to bed.

It was about six months after arriving there that we had an earlier than usual muster of all personnel in the courtyard. There had been a break-out from the guardroom and whoever it was had left two guards in a very bad state and had taken a rifle and ammunition. That evening I found out that it had been my travelling companion, the one who had been marched off to the guardroom after spitting in the fist sergeant's face.

It was now five years since I joined the Foreign Legion. In the beginning it had been very hard at times but it got easier as time went by and I was now speaking very good French and my Arabic was just as good. On top of it all, I had enjoyed joining as they now called me sergeant so I had done well. I was due for some leave and I had submitted a request to spend it at home in England and France so that I could visit my parents and the recruiting sergeant and his family, who were now living in Reims, just north of Paris. Due to my good conduct, my request was granted and I found myself waiting for that old train, only this time going the other way.

I found Mum and Dad were doing very well in their two-up, two-down. Dad was working full time at Brooks Fireworks Factory and Mum had a part-time job in a sweet shop and had joined the WI. With my brothers Ken in the navy, Den in the army and John living away with his partner, there was only Janet left at home so things were running well for them all.

After a week I said that I had to be moving on as I had friends in France who I would like to see. There were a few tears from Mum but Dad shook my hand very firmly, saying, "Thanks, son. You have done us proud."

On my arrival in Reims my friend the recruiting sergeant and his family were very pleased to see me and insisted that I stay with them for a day or two and now that I spoke French we got on very well. I had to tell them everything about the legion and who my commanding officer was and it so happened that they knew of him.

Now their daughter, who was an extremely good-looking young lady of 22, turned out to be a very difficult problem but also a very pleasing one because at every opportunity she insisted on having her wicked way with me much to my enjoyment but not for my conscience because there I was accepting my very good friend's hospitality. She became evermore demanding all the time I was there.

I was more than pleased that the time had arrived for me to take my leave of them and how I managed to look them in the eye as I did I'll never know. I've put that down to my new way of life and of my army training. As ever, leave time always seemed to go so very quickly and I had to start thinking about getting back so once the goodbyes had been said, I made my way to Paris for two days. It was good to be able to speak to the locals in their own tongue.

Two days later I was back at base camp and it took just five minutes for me to forget my leave and get back into my uniform. I was once again Sergeant Leslie James of the French Foreign Legion.

Now time out there in no-man's-land went very slowly and it wore you down, that's if you let it. But if you kept yourself busy it could also go very quickly. I had time to think on one occasion and realised that my leave had been nearly three years before and in that three years I had been promoted once again, this time to first sergeant. So now, at 23, or for the benefit of the legion, 25, I could still see that poster saying "join today" and looking back I could honesty say that if I had my way again I would certainly do just the same because I was enjoying life and was just so very pleased that I had joined.

My speaking French and Arabic had made life a lot easier for the locals and for me because every now and then I liked to go to the marketplace to buy something for Mum and Dad and I greatly enjoy greatly haggling over the price. On one such day I had an encounter with one very beautiful young lady and on my next visit I was looking out for her.

To my surprise, it was she that spoke first with that enchanting voice, a voice that would stay with me for ever.

"Good morning, First Sergeant."

How I persuaded her and the bodyguards to have coffee with me I shall never know, but I did, and while sipping our coffee, very slowly in my case because I truly wanted those moments to last as long as possible, I thought, I'm falling for this beauty. I must have been doing something right because we exchanged names. Her name was Tisha and along with that we agreed to meet once a week at the coffee bar where we both knew the proprietor could be trusted to be discreet, as well as her three giant escorts who waited very patiently outside as long as the door remained open. I think we both enjoyed our meetings because we continued to meet at the coffee bar for several weeks.

I was on my way to my office after such a very pleasant meeting with Tisha to check the daily orders and I saw that I was down for a ten-day patrol in two days' time with a brand new officer from France, a Lieutenant Lewis Chervil. I was to show him the ropes, but it did not work out that way.

On our patrol we were well into our third day out into the desert when we came across a larger than usual caravan about a mile away. There must have been 40 or more camels and they were all very well laden. On stopping, our new and very keen young officer, after looking through his new binoculars, decided to have a closer look and as we got closer the caravan started to move at first to a trot and then, of all things, into a mad run and started to scatter. With our half-track vehicles, we soon had the leader stopped and the rest did not take long to be rounded up. Myself and three men accompanied the lieutenant, who wanted to see the caravan leader for himself and as I had learned their tongue, I was to act as interpreter. It was as we are going forward to talk to the leader that I felt the shot that hit me in the lower part of my left leg before I heard it. I could feel myself falling forward and the pain was incredibly bad. That was when I found out that the sand can be very hard and unrelenting to a mere first sergeant.

Our new lieutenant must have been listening at his training college because he showed that he knew what to do in such an encounter and gave orders that had me behind one of the vehicles and away from any more harm and showed that he had a cool head on his shoulders. On top of that, he had made a name for himself on his first patrol. We had encountered and captured a gun and dope runner of a rather grand size and one of the most wanted men on our list.

I can remember the helicopter arriving and the medic bending over me and saying, "No need to worry now, sir," as I watched him putting the needle in my arm.

I came to in a very bright room looking into the face of a French-speaking angel, who said, "So you're back with us again, sir?"

Apparently I had been flown back to France to a military hospital and had already had an operation on my leg and was told that the surgeon will be seeing me later that day.

When he did arrive, he did not look that happy and started to apologise as soon as he got to my bedside. He told me that they had done their best but he was sorry to say that they'd had to remove some bone and I would be left with a slight limp from the incident.

That was that, who would want a first sergeant with a limp and who would *want* to be a first sergeant with a limp? So after some long and very serious thought, I requested that proceedings for my discharge be set in motion. This was granted on medical grounds and after all the documentation had been completed and my recuperation had me back to health once again, I decided to return to Algeria where I had spent most of my life. I had my rail warrant made out for Bejaia in Algeria as I was hoping to meet up with my Tisha to see how she felt about my disability.

On my arrival in Bejaia I went to our favourite restaurant and coffee bar where we had made a good friend in the owner. I arranged to lodge with him for a few days and he nodded, saying he would pass the word.

The next morning Tisha arrived early, saying, "I have waited for you. I knew you would return to me."

We had such a lot to tell each other and when I told her about the disability, she said that was of no concern as she was just pleased I had come back to her. It was past midday before we decided that I should go with her to her father's house.

Much to my surprise we had been travelling for over three hours deep into the desert and still more surprises lay ahead for us there as there was a larger than usual tent with a great deal of activity with camels coming and going. It was a real beehive of activity. It was then that I met Tisha's father for the first time, Sheik Abijah Yusef Mohammed, a tall man dressed in flowing white robes. His eyes were very bright blue, made more prominent by his well-trimmed beard, which was pure white.

We got on well right from the start and after sitting with him and Tisha in the cool of one of the larger tents at a table of sweet meats and black sweet coffee, and with me answering a great deal of questions from the sheik, which was to be expected, he stood up smiling and said, "Now a thousand pardons, if you will please excuse me for I go for my rest," and with a slight bow he left us.

It was then that Tisha told me all about her father and his followers, whom he treated as family, and that he had a great deal of land that the oil companies were looking to buy it from him. But he had no need of money as he just happened to be a very wealthy man. I started to feel very uneasy with this news because I could not even start to think about ever being able to keep my lovely Tisha in the same way as her father.

That evening after our delicious meal of goat meat with rice and a delicacy of fresh fruits, Tisha's father said, "My daughter I need to talk to Leslie alone. Come, my son, let's walk."

We walked in silence. It was a strange feeling as not more than ten yards behind us at all the times was the sheik's bodyguard of six well-armed men. Even so, we had only gone a few yards, when it was I that broke the silence by bursting out and saying, "Sir, I would like to marry your daughter."

With a big smile and at the same time putting his arm round my shoulders, he replied, "So be it. It's Allah's will, but you must make an old man happy by doing just one thing for me and all will be well."

"Anything, sir" I replied.

I was shocked by his reply. "You must come and work for me at Mohammed's Trading Company."

"Sir, it would give me great deal of pleasure to do so," and with that he gave me a big hug and we shook hands.

That's when my world changed as I had become one of the family and no matter how I tried, everything was done for me. The clothing I stood up in was taken from me and I was bathed by women of all ages, who were having the time of there lives pointing at me and giggling among themselves giving not a thought for my blushes or to the fact that I understood everything word they said. They then dressed me in silks just like the sheik himself. I liked what was happening to me.

In six weeks Tisha and I were married in the tradition of the land and were on our way to Europe and England for our honeymoon.

Our honeymoon went very well and very quickly. We spent a pleasant time with my mum and dad in England, who were completely happy that I had found someone so beautiful. We even managed to sleep in my old bed, but only for the one night, and then it was on to the Arioso Hotel in Paris to meet my old recruiting sergeant and his wife. The troublesome daughter had flown the nest and was now married with a family of her own, thank goodness.

Then we went on to visit Rome staying at the Cavalieri Waldorf and then the Bellasera Hotel in Naples. It was whilst in Naples that the telegram arrived asking us to return to Tisha's father in Bejaia.

We arrived feeling very anxious the very next day, not knowing what to expect, but our arrival coincided with another load of hard-talking salesmen from the oil companies and we found out they had been pestering the sheik once again trying to get him to sell his land.

Tisha and I managed to get rid of them with the promise of a further meeting with them in one week's time. It was then that Tisha's father asked Tisha and I to go with him to his private quarters and he informed us that he was tired of all the pressure that was being forced on him by the oil companies.

Then looking at me he said, "My son, I would like you to take over and look after my interest so that I can live in peace among my friends."

"It's a great honour that you place on me but what of your sons and of Tisha's interests?"

It was then that I learned that his wife had died in childbirth while given birth to Tisha and Allah had not granted him any sons. He continued by saying, "So you see, you are my son."

I looked at Tisha, who gave a slight nod I looked at the old chap saying that I would be very proud and honoured by his very generous offer and that I would see that his every wish would be fulfilled."

My first task as the new managing director came one week later when, as expected, the oil company land grabbers had arrived as arranged, seeking my father-in-law. After having my secretary explain the situation to them and that of the changes that had taken place, I gave them a short spell to take it all in and talk it over amongst themselves and then with Tisha at my side, we walked into my office, which was in a large tent with a great many rugs and twice as many cushions scattered around.

"Well, gentlemen, what is it you want of me?"

They all started to talk and wave their arms at me at the same time. I held my hand up until they had all stopped and then told them that I had no intention of selling the land but if they would come back in a month's time with a proposal for leasing the land, I would then contact the company who had, in my opinion, submitted the best proposal. I could see they certainly did not like the outcome of this meeting but leave they did.

I reported to the sheik, who listened and then said, "You have done very well, my son. Allah has given me my son who has taken a great weight off this old man's shoulders. But please remember, you do not have to report to me because my problems are now your problems. I would like to have peace in my remaining few years.

It had now been six years since I married Tisha and we have three fine children – two boys called Abijan and Mohammed, along with our lovely daughter, Tisha. We still lived with the sheik but the compound is that much larger and now, just lately, the sheik had given us a great deal of concern regarding his health. But he would not leave his home so I had arranged for a medical team to stay at the compound with all the equipment they needed and a helicopter on standby all the time. But alas, my friend and father-in-law called Tisha and I to his quarters once again, said his goodbyes and then he passed away very peacefully that night with us at his bedside.

The next morning, according to the custom, his friends formed a caravan and carried out his last wish that he be buried in an unmarked grave inside his land, we found a spot of rolling sand hills leading to an oasis with swaying palm trees and laid him to rest. All those present, quietly and with a great deal of respect, walked away, but Tisha and I looked back only to see that the ever-blowing wind had already moved the sand and it was hard to find any trace of us ever being there. We both lowered our heads and hand in hand said a silent prayer for our great loss.

The next morning two Land Rovers arrived, which was a surprise for Tisha and I as it was a visit from the sheik's solicitors from Mestghanem, a coastal town west of Algiers. How they knew of the sheik's death so quickly we will never know, but in a way they had good news for us both. The sheik had left his entire estate, lands and wealth to Tisha and I to share. The only thing was that Tisha being a woman, she was not the head of the family and everything was in my name.

That evening Tisha and I had a talk and decided that with all this great fortune we should start to take it easy and do something with it, so we called the solicitors back and arranged for the two boys, who had good results from their English education at Cambridge University and our daughter, now out of finishing school, to look after our interests by running the estate on our behalf.

Now Tisha had been on about living away from the sand and would like to live somewhere where it was green so that was how we find ourselves living on a country estate in Surrey, just south of Box Hill, which is not that far from Epsom and its famous horse racing track where I have interest in one of the stables. We also have an apartment in London overlooking Hyde Park. Even with all this luxury, we both love to go back to our friends and enjoy the peaceful surrounds of the blowing sands but we are enjoying life to the full now. And all this from a poster saying "You may join the Foreign Legion here".

Homecoming

It was only last night that I landed at London's Heathrow Airport flying in from Egypt and now I'm enjoying a lazy lie-in at my parents' home. It had been of my own choosing to end my army career of eight good years, but lying there I had time to think, have I made the right decision to leave? But then I do have six months to make my mind up, so I got up had a shower and shaved. The reflection in the mirror was of a well-tanned man of 27 years old, 5ft 8ins tall with hazel eyes, light brown hair and a stockily built body, with muscle built by eight years army service. I felt very pleased with what I saw.

Mum insisted that I had a full English breakfast, not forgetting the black pudding, and it was then that I told her I was just going to pop round to see Jane. I was hoping for a spot of relaxation time with our Jane.

Mum stopped me as I was going out of the door and said, "Mind how you go, son. Don't do anything rash." Strange words coming from Mum, so with a bit of a spring in my step, I headed for Jane's.

As I remembered, all her letters over the last three years had been warm and loving with S.W.A L.K on the back of the envelopes. It felt good to be seeing Jane again. I knocked on the door and it was her mother who opened the door. She just stood looking at me and looking very flustered, but managed to call out, "Jane, it's Leslie to see you!"

Now Jane, as I remember her, was a tall, very lovely looking blond with a figure to die for. Well, she was still tall and blond but she was very unkempt and dirty looking. She was also carrying a young one in her arms of about a year old and to top it all, she was also very heavily pregnant again. It was not the Jane who I had left behind. My bubble had burst, I could not believe in what I was seeing and Jane she did not even try to say anything.

I was completely stunned and all I could find to say was, "Well, I can see you have been busy," and with that I just turned and left her standing there.

It was then that Mum's words come back to me, she must have known. The spring in my step had gone and with my head down I started to walk back towards Mum's. But all my luck had not completely left me because standing outside her house was Pat. Now Pat had been a good friend of mine for a very long time.

"Hello, lover boy!" she said.

Boy, oh boy, was I pleased to see her. Pat was a year older than me but she was another one with the perfect body and her red hair showed off her pale, creamy skin. She was just one great lady.

She said, "Come in and say hello to Mum and Dad, they will be pleased to see you."

So in I go, shaking hands with her dad and being hugged by her mum and they both said, "It's nice to see you home again. I bet your mum's pleased to have you home again."

After a few more pleasantries I said very Politely, "I can see you're going out so I had better leave so that you can be on your way."

"No," said Mrs Wilson. "Stay and talk to Pat, I'm sure you both have lots of news to tell as you've have not seen each other for a very long time." And with that they both said, "Thanks for calling in to see us," and left. But Mrs

Wilson came back and said to Pat, "Don't forget about next Saturday."

I looked at Pat and said, "What's that all about?"

She turned away, Saying, "I'll tell you later."

With Mum and Dad out of sight, she took my hand and led me to her bedroom. It had not changed since the last time I had been there and for the next hour or so it became very steamy and extremely enjoyable. She had always been very demanding and the groaning and continually asking for more was as I remembered it. We lay there naked and exhausted. She was just lying there taking in deep breaths, her naked body was a sight that no man could resist so I lay with her again and we started all over again, only this time we moaned together until we both collapsed exhausted on the bed.

After we had both got our breath back, I asked what her mother had meant when she had said "Remember next week".

"Oh, that! I'm getting married in two weeks' time."

I don't know where I got the energy from but I managed to jump off the bed, staring at Pat. She just led there and giggled and then said, "You do look funny standing there all naked and spent."

We both started to laugh and I fell back onto the bed where we lay in each other's arms kissing and caressing each other as we both realised that we did not have the energy for anything else.

After a while we finally got dressed and went for a walk over the adjoining farm's mint fields, just like the old days where we had in the past spent many a passionate moment. They being the good old times in each other's company.

Thanks to the army I have a very healthy bank account so I had no need to rush to find employment but I did need some new civvies and that was the reason for my looking in the men's shops in Sutton High Street. That was when I heard someone say, "Hi, Leslie! What in the heck you doing in Sutton?"

It was my old buddy Harry Short, a 6ft 4ins tall and a very handsome guy, and due to his size he had picked up the nickname of Tiny. Unfortunately, he was badly hurt while we were serving in Northern Ireland and he had been discharged with a pension and now lived and worked in Carshalton. After a pint or two at the local White Horse Hotel, we had exchanged all the latest gossip and why I was in Sutton and it was while we were heading along the shops towards Tiny's home to meet his wife and family that I stopped to have a look in the Fifty Bob Taylor's on the corner of West Street; the same West Street where I had lived for the first part of my life. That's when I noticed the old chap in the window of the butcher's shop sticking up a notice "Driver wanted for light van deliveries. Early morning start required. Good wages for the right person."

Something was telling me that this was for me, even knowing that I had no need to start working just now. I stood looking for a bit and then tapped on the window, pointing at the advert. The old chap opened the door but now that he was standing upright he did not look so old, just very tired maybe and with a worried look, but he did have a very pleasant smile.

He said, "Can I help you?"

"It's about the job in the window," I replied. "Can you tell me more about it?"

After he'd explained the job and I'd given him my situation and how I happened to be in the area, too eagerly, I thought, he said the job was mine for the taking and when could I start?

I had already come to realise that he needed a driver very badly and so with tongue in cheek I said I could start the next day, Wednesday for full week's money!

After a short hesitation, he said, "You have a deal."

We shook hands and I knew I had made a new friend. That's how I started my first temporary appointment after leaving the army.

The next day, promptly at 0600 hrs on my arrival at the shop, I had a good look round both the shop and the cutting area. There were four others plus the old fellow working hard at it so I called out "Good morning to you! My name is Leslie, I'm the new van driver."

I received a chorus of acknowledgement from them all but I did notice that they did not stop working and I could see the look of relief on the old chap's face! I looked around and spotted the pile of trays fully filled with assorted meats.

"Are these the trays for delivery?" I asked. "And how do we go about loading them, Bert?"

The old chap said, "It's best I help you today and show you the route we take."

The van was a very old Bedford Bullnose, 15cwt, which had seen many better days. I looked over at Bert, saying, "That van don't look too good. Are you sure it's okay for the job?"

After loading the trays I walked around this very old Bedford van taking a good look at the springs. We were surely well and truly overloaded. Well, it was my first day so I kept quiet, but even so, it was a very dangerous load and on top that a great deal of blood was running out of the holes in the floor and the back doors.

We were ready for the off; I pulled the piece of string sticking out of the dashboard, which, as I was informed, was the starter connection, but not even a groan the battery – it was completely flat. That put Bert into a flap but with a bit of luck his car was close by and I was able to change the battery over with the one out of his car and this time we started off, having to use a lot of power and first gear to even get the darn thing moving on what was to be one of the most hysterical, dangerous and very enlightening drives of my life.

Loss of power from the clapped out engine when needed; both passenger and driver seats not really secured; horn button missing; windscreen wipers not working and a metal noise coming from all four wheels when the brakes were applied, telling me the brake pads required replacement.

On our return there was no need to say anything because Bert had been so badly scared when he had to put a tray under the back wheel to stop the van from running back down one of the many hills we had encountered due to the fact that when I applied the handbrake it had come away in my hand. As soon as we got back, Bert phoned head office and explained the situation and was given permission to get a replacement. I put the battery back into his car and we both went to Croydon car sales and came away with a nearly new Ford Transit. From then on deliveries went like clockwork.

I washed the inside of the van every day with plenty of Dettol and made a point of maintaining it as well. It turned out to be a great job; I was on my own most of the time and an early start meant an early finish, which was to my liking. But at times I gave Stan a hand in the shop serving, which boosted my pay packet and it was also great fun as I was able to give the customers, mostly the ladies, plenty of cheek. Some of them tried calling my bluff, "I'm yours, just hope you can deliver on time, say one o'clock" or "Bring my sausages round about one o'clock and let's see if I can get more than eight to the pound, lover boy". I never let the customers down and met all the challenges with the greatest of pleasure and full satisfaction was given to all that tried calling my bluff.

I'd been working there for three weeks when Bert asked to see me in the office. I thought it was the "tin tack" for being just too cheeky to the lady customers, but he said, "Let's go out in the van and fill it up ready for the next day's run." But he knew I always did that on my return to the shop, so we drove up to the garage and I made a point of checking the vans tyres for wear and tear and put some air in. It was then that he asked me how I felt about doing a delivery for the big boss.

"If it's legal, I'm your man," I replied and added, "I take it will be made worth my while?"

It was then that we agreed on a bonus of cash in hand at the end of each week. My first "big boss run" was the very next day to a golf club in Chipstead; just a load of meat for the restaurant, or so I thought!

As previously instructed, I was to park in the car park at the back of the hotel and just sit tight. The hotel chief, who was the real "Mr Big" must be the very man who was walking towards me I knew from the very first moment I saw him that he was a "nine bob note".

He came over and sat in the cab, smelling very strongly of body perfume, and asked me if I knew the Epsom and Ewell area.

"Yes, I've lived in this area all my life," I said.

"That's good. Here are the two addresses I would like you to deliver to. Most of your load to this address," and at the same time handing me a piece of paper with the two addresses and the small parcel of meat for the other address.

The first stop was a hotel close to the Epsom Race Track where a ten pound note was discretely tucked into my top pocket as soon as the delivery was completed. I then realised that was my reward for not asking questions. The next delivery was a private house in Epsom. I knocked on the door and a very attractive young lady of about 27, the same age as myself, said, "Hello, are you from the chief?"

"Yes, that's right," I replied. "I have a small parcel of meat for you."

That low husky voice said, "Would you be a dear and please put it in the freezer for me?"

I could not stop looking at her and I was hoping she would not notice. She was really beautiful. She returned from another part of the house and asked if I would like a cup of tea or coffee.

I said, "I could do with drink of some kind, maybe an orange or lemonade as I don't drink tea or coffee,"

She said, once again in that low husky voice, "I have some Coca-Cola, would that be all right?"

"That would be fine," I replied.

So we both sat there sipping our drinks. I felt very comfortable sitting there with her and it was not long before I told her my story of how I had joined the company having just left the army and that my name was Leslie. She did not say a great deal about herself, only that her name was Rachel and she did not get out a great deal and was very lonely most of the time as her husband had other interests.

"You have met him, he's the chief that you spoke to earlier."

Now I got the picture; I could not let an opportunity like this to slip through my fingers and said, "Well, if you like, I would be more than pleased to take you out at any time. I'll be at the shop awaiting your call." I said, "Thanks for the drink, I had better get back to the shop now as Bert will start worrying."

She asked me to give Bert her love and a kiss, which she planted very firmly on my cheek.

I said, "Bert is a very lucky man."

On my return to the shop, I found Bert in his office. I went over and kissed him on the cheek and said, "Rachel sends her love, you sly old dog."

He went completely scarlet and I found out later that he had soft spot for her. He then told me there was a message for me from Rachel and would I please ring this number. In the circumstances, I could not use the office phone so I made the excuse to go to the sweet shop to get a box of chocolates for my mum. There was a public telephone box outside. We arranged to meet that same afternoon; she would pick me up at the London Road car park at Nonesuch Park Gardens.

I was early and waiting at the stated time when Rachel arrived in a Red Honda Accord. She did look marvellous and I was thinking, you lucky devil, Leslie, and she said, "Let's go somewhere quiet so that we can have a chat."

I said, "How about the King's Head Hotel off the Dorking bypass?"

We sat in silence until we arrived and then Rachel twisted in her seat lent over a kissed me very passionately. I responded with just as much passion and I'm sure we both enjoyed it very much. The hotel was empty, just as we had hoped, but we had a hard time shaking off the barman who wanted to talk. We made plans for the following weekend for as it worked out, the husband had a big reception to supervise over at his place of work. He had already told Rachel that he would not be home for the weekend. I said I would get a move on with my deliveries and would meet her at Epsom clock tower about 1.30.

I've never known a week to go so slowly. I told Bert I had an appointment that weekend and would like to get away sharp on Friday. He gave me a funny look and said, "Take good care of her. She deserves someone like you."

Right on time, the red Honda arrived and we set off towards Dorking.

I said, "Where are we going?"

With a big grin, which turned into a very beautiful smile, she said, "Sit back and enjoy the ride."

I did just that, the A29 onto the Brighton road, and a short time later we pulled up on the forecourt of The Grand Hotel. Rachel gave the keys to the porter and said, "Now remember, this is my treat and I want you to enjoy your stay because I know I'm going to." With that she held my hand and said, "Come on, let's have a good time."

The hotel foyer was crowded but it did not take very long before we were in our suite; one large sitting room, a bathroom with a large shower with all the modern fittings and the bedroom had this very large king-size bed. The view from the balcony was great, you could see the pier and sea, giving a musical sound as it rolled back across the shingle. It was just prefect, but it was the bed which had my full attention at that moment because lying there was Rachel with that beautiful smile, partly dressed and beckoning to me to join her. I undressed as quickly as I could.

She looked so lovely and I needed no beckoning and I joined those welcoming arms in what turned out to be a real humdinger of a session; no groaning from Rachel, like the others, but a continual purring like a very happy cat and me, I felt like a very happy puppy with a bag of bones.

The next morning we had our shower together, which led to another serious session of exotic lovemaking, there seemed to have no end to our needs for each other. Later we ordered room service for a late breakfast with Champagne. We were both ravenous and enjoyed the full English. After separate showers we got dressed and went for a walk along the promenade but the day had started wet and windy so we hastily returned to the hotel and the four-poster was the location for a lot more action once again. Once more we had exhausted ourselves and we just lay there caressing and touching, enjoying each other's company. We decided to go out for a meal that night, only this time we had separate showers.

We took a taxi to a very quaint restaurant in Rottingdean and had a very nice meal with an excellent bottle of red wine that went down very well. We were both just sipping the last of the wine and both of us were in deep thought as we knew that tomorrow we must return to normality once again.

I glanced up only to see that there were tears in Rachel's eyes. I reached over and squeezed her hand, saying, "Don't cry, my lovely. There can be other times."

We paid the bill and asked for a taxi. On our arrival at the hotel we sat in the lounge and talked things over and decided to leave later that night but back in our room Rachel just broke down and cried. I just did not know how to say it's back to normality tomorrow, my lovely, but I did because I knew that both of us did not want this weekend to end but both our situations in the real world did not allow us to continue as we would have liked.

After talking it over we said it would be better for us to leave tonight. We did what packing was to be done and phoned the reception desk to have our account ready as we would be leaving in two hours. The four-poster bed was a great temptation and one that we could not resist and we once more had a period of great satisfaction in each other's capabilities, enjoying the remaining time we had.

The red Honda was waiting for us when we had completed the check out and the journey back was as quiet as the one down. That was until Rachel decided to stop and kissed me, saying, "Thank you for a great weekend. I thought I detected a hint of finality in her voice but she knew how to kiss and at the moment I could only think of giving back as good as I was receiving.

As we continued along the A23 we passed a bus and I said, "If you stop at next bus stop ahead, I can catch that bus and that means you don't have to take me to Epsom." After another lingering kiss, I said, "Ring the shop."

I flagged the bus to stop and after sitting down I looked out the window but could not see any sign of the Honda. When I arrived back at Mum and Dad's, Mum took one look at me and said, whatever have you been up to? You look so tired."

I kissed her on top of her head and said, "That's why I'm going straight to bed." As I passed Dad I gave him a wink and got a smile and a nod in return.

The next morning I arrived at the shop on time only to find Bert in tears. He'd had a phone call from Rachel who told him that her husband the pig had badly beaten her the night before. He looked over at me, saying, "I'll be coming with you this morning. I've a call to make."

On arrival at the school I explained to the cooks that I had the boss man with me so we had to cut out the tea and chat time. They all played along but I still got a grope from two of them. We did the round in half the normal time and on the way round I thought it was only fair to tell Bert about the weekend I had spent with Rachel.

He said, "I thought that was it, but I don't blame you one little bit and I'm glad she has found some happiness from that pig she married."

We arrived at Rachel's house and took a small parcel of meat in. When she opened the door Bert took one look and fell to his knees and cried like a baby. She picked him up and comforted him. She looked round at me, saying, "I've told him nothing and every moment of that lovely weekend was worth it, so don't worry about it. I'll phone the shop when the bruising has gone."

Bert and I very reluctantly left Rachel and we drove up to the racecourse and parked the van. I looked over at Bert and said, "I want to know what he gets up to, where he goes, who goes with him and what time he starts and finishes work and anything that will help me take care of things." Bert looked over at me and said he would do his best. With that we drove back to the shop. I parked up and slowly walked home and lay on my bed doing some thinking.

The next morning Bert was true to his word and had even done better than his best because now I had everything I needed. I told Bert that the van would be of help for a couple of days and he just nodded and said "Be careful."

That same night I parked the van a short distance from the hotel, the pig's place of work, I then walked to the back of the hotel where I had a good view of the car park and the rear entrance. The Honda was parked there so he must still be using Rachel's car. I did not have to wait that long when the door opened and the pig came out and walked towards the Honda. I noted all this and what cover there was because I intended to return the next night.

The next day I purchased a small car blanket and once again that night I parked the van in the same place and made my way to the back of the hotel and waited for that door to open, only this time I stood well back in the shadow. I did not have that long to wait as the door opened and as usual the pig walked towards the Honda. As he went passed I stepped out, putting blanket over his head and pulling him down to the ground. He screamed out but the blanket muffed it and I laid into him first with my fist and then with both boots. He tried to shout but my boot filled his mouth I then planted my boot as hard as I could into his privates. He screamed but the blanket was doing its job and muffled any sound. He just led there very still, but moaning. I knew it was a cowardly attack and was not proud of it, but I could not take the chance of him seeing me. Any how, it was no more than he deserved for the attack he had carried out on Rachel.

I left him with the blanket still covering his head but still moaning and walked slowly away and back to the van and then slowly drove back home.

The next morning I arrived at the shop as usual only to find it was all closed up, no cutters and no Bert, so I parked the van at the back in the yard and started to walk home. The walk would do me good, give me time to think, but while passing the local garage I noticed Bert in his car.

He beckoned me over and said, "Leslie, get in. I've been waiting for you. Let's get away from here." He sped away like he was being followed and did not stop until we found an empty car park on Belmont Downs. Apparently he'd had a phone call from Rachel who had told him that the pig was in hospital with a policeman sitting at his bedside and thanked him for all he had done for her in the past. She also said to tell me to lay low for a bit and that she would never forget me and at the same time advised Bert to get out as quickly as he could as due to the attack, the police were now making enquiries into why it took place and into the company books.

When he'd asked her for an address, she said, "Sorry, I don't want you getting mixed up in this. But don't worry, I will contact you."

So that's how it worked out and that was the last we both saw or heard of Rachel since the day we called at her house. She never did make contact and I've since had time to think and I explained the situation to Mum and Dad.

I said, "I'll be writing to my commanding officer in Egypt."

I posted the letter the same day. I took Mum and Dad out to a show and a dinner and for Dad's sake we went to the Lord Nelson on Sunday morning where we had a couple of pints but we made sure we did not arrive back late for Mum's Sunday dinner of roast lamb with all the trimmings. On our arrival at home, I could see Bert's car parked outside the drive. I said to Dad, "A friend of mine. I'll just have a word."

That was when he told me that the company managing director and the chief, Rachel's husband, had all been arrested on several charges but had later been released pending some serious corruption charges to be heard at a later date.

Dad and I were laying the table when the doorbell rang; it was Mr Wilson, Pat's father, with an invitation for Mum and Dad to visit Pat's new house in Dorking the next day. When he saw me, he said, "Why don't you come as well, Leslie? I'm sure Pat would love to see you." We all gladly accepted. "We will be leaving at ten o'clock, so see you all tomorrow, then."

We then talked about tomorrow's visit as we were enjoying one of Mum's very special Sunday dinners. After helping to clear away the dishes, I said, "Just going for a walk to get some air."

As I went around the farm fields, I could not but help but think of Pat. I was looking forward to seeing her again.

After a very sunny and pleasant journey, on our arrival Pat was standing at the top of a flight steeps in bright sunlight in front of the very impressive oak door of a very large house, which was standing in lot of ground. But Pat had fulfilled part of her dream and got what she had always wanted, all that was lacking was her stage career that she had always wanted. But then her husband did just happen to be a film director, who at that moment in time was in Hollywood.

When she saw me she said, "My, my! This is a pleasant surprise! How are you keeping, lover boy?"

That's when her mum said, "You had better not let Harry hear you say that."

Mr Wilson, Reg, said, "Come on, Jack, I'll show you the grounds and pond."

Mrs Wilson, Jill, said, "Come on, Florrie, I'll show you the house."

With that Pat said, "Well, come on, Leslie. I'll show you the stables."

We all set off but not before Jill looked at Pat and said, "When is Harry due back?" A subtle way of saying behave yourself.

Pat said, "He hasn't said but he will ring a day or two before anyhow." So off we went on our separate ways.

I said to Pat, "You know your mother knows what we get up to?"

Pat said, "I've thought that but she has never said anything, but never mind, let's just enjoy ourselves."

We did just that and it's a wonder everyone within a mile did not know because Pat still moans, but now a great deal louder! We were walking in the grounds when Pat asked, "Could you get down tomorrow? I'll meet you at Epsom clock tower."

I said "Yes" at the same time and it started me thinking of Rachel and Bert as I never did hear any more news of either of them.

Pat arrived on time and we drove to the house in what seemed a record time, as soon as we got inside the door she took my hand and led the way to the bedroom. It was more palatial and twice the size with a large four-poster bed and a modern ensuite. Much better than her room at her parents' house. But she had not forgotten what takes place in one and we both remembered very quickly.

We had a great time and she said, "If only you had been a film director."

I then told her of my decision to rejoin the army, but not the reason why, and that I was awaiting my orders. That's when Pat said, "Let's have a day or two together, just so that I can always think of you from time to time. Please, let's go next week. I'll make all the arrangements and phone you at your mum's, please, lover boy, say yes. Just one more day, one more time before you go back."

I could not find it in me to refuse her and it was the next evening when she rang saying all the arrangements had been made and she would meet me once again at Epsom clock tower at ten o'clock the next day.

On the dot of ten o'clock Pat arrived looking as always very cool and very beautiful in her gleaming silver and black Bentley and I realised that I could be just that bit fond of my Pat and I too was looking forward to just once more and this weekend must be a good one.

We stayed at The Ritz Hotel in Eastbourne for three days and three nights and they were three days and nights that would be remembered by the two of us for a very long time, or even always.

It was two weeks later when the letter arrived from Egypt. I was to report to Shorncliffe Training Camp and Dispersal Centre in Kent in ten days' time. Mum arranged to have all my uniform dry cleaned and Dad said he would like to do my boots and webbing brass, so between the three of us I was ready to go with three days to spare. Another theatre outing for Mum and Dad and this time I invited Pat's Mum and Dad as well and decided to report back two days early. So the following day with a lot of tears from Mum and Dad all red eyed and Mr and Mrs Wilson with big hugs and hand shaking, it was a very nice send off. I climbed into the taxi and with my letter of recall safely in my pocket and with mixed emotions, I managed to say to the driver "Waterloo Station, please."

The RTO at Waterloo Station in London was an old sergeant with rows of campaign ribbons on his chest and on reading the letter he issued me with the required travel warrant and walked with me to the train, making sure that I got a seat. He then shook my hand and said, "Glad to have you back, Sergeant Major. I'll be letting Shorncliffe know you're coming."

The train was full mainly with army personnel and they all seemed to be going to Shorncliffe, but seeing as my seat had been found for me I had time to take stock of my travelling companions. Most of them had been drinking and talking quite freely and they had been on embarkation leave.

It was halfway into the journey when the train stopped at Swanley Station in Kent where a young woman, accompanied by a small boy in her arms and a very large suitcase, struggled to find a seat. I gave her mine and made room for the suitcase. Apparently she was going to join her husband at Shorncliffe who was a member of the permanent staff in the dispatch office at the camp.

On reaching Shorncliffe Station, I was giving her a helping hand when her husband arrived. After he had greeted his wife and son, it was his wife Mary who said, "Barry, this is Sergeant Major James. He gave me his seat and helped me with the case."

Barry, who was a sergeant, said, "Very grateful for your help, sir. It's funny we should meet like this as I have been given special instructions about you and was to locate you as soon as you arrived. There should be a car here for you and you're getting the full treatment! That's the driver, I'll go and get him."

The car pulled alongside and I said, "If we are all going to the same destination you might as well come with me and then you won't lose me." With that we all had a good laugh and piled into the car, not forgetting the suitcase.

The next morning I reported to the camp office only to find Barry all ready at work.

"Good morning, Sergeant Major. Did you have a good night?"

"Yes, thank you, but I cannot get used to having women sharing the same quarters as men."

There was a shout for Sergeant Godfrey and Barry stood up and replied, "Yes sir." Now I knew his name.

He returned from the office and said, "Would you please come this way, Sergeant Major? The CO will see you now."

It was then I was informed that there was a delay at the moment and I was to make myself available in the sergeant's mess and if I wished to leave the camp at any time I was to leave an address or a location with Sergeant Godfrey.

On leaving the office Barry called out, "Care for a drink, Sergeant Major?"

"That would be very nice," I replied, so we went to the permanent staff sergeant's mess where Barry picked a table well away from the rest of the occupants and after a good look around said, "Leslie, how would you like to travel back to Egypt?"

"Have I got a choice?" I replied.

"Well, it's like this, we do have some places on air flights which will take you back to your unit in three days, or if you prefer by ship, which will take three or four weeks, which will also get you acclimatised once again to the heat. Plus this way will mean that you could be doing me a good turn."

"Then I'll take the slower way, please," was my reply.

With one great big smile on his face, he said, "So be it. Get yourself ready to meet your travelling companions tomorrow at 10.00 outside the office. I hope we shall still be friends at 10.30!" and he would not enlighten me as to what to expect.

The next morning I arrived ten minutes early to have a word with Barry only to find him hard at work with two male sergeants, one female sergeant major and three female sergeants, all talking to him at once. He spotted me and said in a rather loud voice, "Sergeant Major James, these are the NCOs and the personnel outside who are, as from now, your responsibility." The sergeant major and the sergeants all stopped talking.

I walked over to them and said, "Right outside. Fall in with your respective details and wait for me."

They all made for the door except the sergeant major, who said, "You don't expect me to stand with that lot, do you?"

I looked at her eye to eye. "Yes, I do expect you to stand with your detail. You are now under my command and yes, when I give an order you will do as you are told. Now, go outside and stand with your unit."

She stormed out of the office saying what sounded like "big pig" and took up her position at the head of the ATS unit. The look from Barry said "thank you", and you could see the relief in his eyes and we both had a smile on our faces. He then told me that I would be on my way the next day and it had been arranged for transport to be outside the office at 0630 hrs as we would be going by train to Dover and would be on board ship the same day.

All in the same breath he said, "Mary and I were wondering if you would like to have dinner with us tonight at our home."

My reply was that I would be delighted. We shook hands and I went outside. I called the NCOs and told them the news and that they were to be on parade with their detail outside this office at 0630 hrs ready to go to the station. From now and until then they could please themselves but they were not to leave the camp.

The dinner at the Godfreys was a great success and I got to know that Barry hated his job at the office. I said I would have a word with my CO on my return to the regiment.

The next morning everyone was on parade with the exception of one cook out of the girls of the ATS detachment, who had gone AWOL. I could only see three trucks and it was then that Sergeant Godfrey informed me that they were for the detachments' kit and all personnel would have to march to the station. That was when my second problem presented itself; the ATS sergeant major and one of her sergeants said they would get a taxi to the station as they did not want to march with the rest of us.

That was the first time I saw red and nearly lost my temper but I could see that would not be the answer so I then called all the NCOs together and told them that like it or not, they would be marching to the station in front of their respectful detachments and that I would not tolerate any more questioning of my orders or stand having my authority questioned.

"As from now on, you will do as you are told," and that's how 160 souls set off for Egypt, doing a three-mile march through the streets of Dover at seven o'clock in the morning behind their respected NCOs.

The next morning we were well down the English Channel and as previously arranged, I met the NCOs in the forward lounge. I could see that all was not well; the navy had not considered that 30 of this detachment were women.

I had a talk to the number two, who agreed that changes had to be made. It was therefore arranged that the ATS would take berths on number three deck; that meant there would be plenty of room for the men. My luck was still holding out due to Barry and I had a cabin on number two deck. The ATS sergeant major and her two sergeants shared another along the same deck.

After the evening meal I was out on deck just looking out towards the coastline, which must have been Cherbourg, enjoying the relaxation this time of the day gave me, when a pleasant voice said, "Good evening to you, Sergeant Major."

At first I wasn't very pleased at having my free time interrupted, but seeing that it was one of the ATS sergeants, I replied, "Yes, it's a great time of the day. Are you on your own?"

"Oh, yes," she said. "I've no time for what they get up to and I could not stand it any longer so I'll give them an hour and they will both be passed out on one of the beds."

I just did not think much of what she had said until two days later, but for now I asked her if she would like to walk around the decks. We did just that, meeting many of the other passengers and having a chat to some of them. It was the remark of one of the girls that set me thinking.

"Hi, Sergeant. How are the lovers? Still drunk as skunks?" she asked.

"Watch your tongue!" Rhoda Williams replied, but it did not stop all the girls in the area from having a good laugh.

We stopped at the bow of the ship and exchanged first names.

I said, "If you're around about the same time tomorrow I would love to walk with you, Rhoda."

The reply was, "I'd be delighted, Leslie. See you at 7.00, port side amidships. Goodnight."

I went back to my cabin and led on my bunk thinking of the girl's remark about "the lovers".

The next morning I had words with the number one, expressed my concern and requested that a parade of the girls on the subject of "What to expect in Egypt" was arranged for the next day.

Two o'clock next day the ATS detachment was assembled in the main restaurant with the exception of the sergeant major and one sergeant, who was said to be too ill to attend. I informed the ship's medical officer, who made a visit to their cabin. His report when made to the captain was unfavourable and I was summoned to the captain's cabin and received a very strong telling off for not keeping a better eye on things. He then asked what I intended to do about it?

I replied that having read the medical officer's report, on arrival at our destination I would hand them over to the Military Police for their very bad conduct. In the meantime I would arrange with the remaining sergeant to take over the duties of the sergeant major and with his permission see that the two in question were separated and confined to separate cabins for the remaining journey.

The captain said, "That sounds like the right thing to do, but keep an eye on them."

I informed Rhoda, Sergeant Williams, who said, "Thanks, thanks very much! That lot are going to be one hell of a handful, but don't worry, I'll sort them out."

We had our stroll around the deck as usual and this time I plucked up the courage to kiss her. Much to my surprise she responded with some passion and then said, "I think we had better say goodnight, Sergeant Major," giving me a peck on the cheek.

We had passed Malta a couple of nights back so I passed the word that all personnel had better start getting packed ready for disembarkation prior to our arrival at Port Said. In 36 hours' time I had a meeting with the ship's number one who informed me that the two in confinement were both still very violent and uncivil and could not be spoken to, so it was arranged that they should be taken off after the others had landed.

That night I met Rhoda as usual and we had a hard time finding a place to be on our own. I was about to suggest that we used my cabin when Rhoda said, "Come on, let's go to your cabin."

A lot kissing and fondling went on but we went no further as we both had to make the rounds to see that everything would be ready for a very early morning start.

We docked at three in the morning and after a good breakfast we started to disembark at six o'clock. The ATS went first, straight onto the waiting train, followed by the REME and signal detachments and then the remaining troops. It was then that things went wrong as in full sight of everyone, the two ATS were being helped from their confinement, both in handcuffs, looking a real mess and shouting and swearing. The vocabulary coming from them was better than any docker's. They were being assisted by some very big MPs, which was not what we had planned but it was a very good lesson for all the others to remember.

On our arrival at Ismailia on the Suez Canal about halfway into our journey, one half of the signal detachment and half the REME disembarked. The remaining personnel were issued with haversack rations and plenty of strong tea and then once more we set off on a very hot and dusty journey.

On our arrival at Suez we were met by the regimental duty officer, who looked very young for a full lieutenant, with transport supplied by the 30th Company of the RACS and what looked like half the regiment as escorts. It appeared that some locals and members of the police had taken a dislike to us being in Egypt, especially their part of it which just happen to be Suez. Once I could see all was well with my detachment, once again I reported to the duty officer.

He looked very puzzled and said, "Don't know what the hell we are going to do with the women! But never mind that, Sergeant Major, you are to report to the CO right away. You had better take that jeep and two men."

Arriving at the camp I could see that all was just the same as when I had left it five months before. The CO must have seen me arrive because as soon as I stepped onto the office veranda he called, "In the office, Sergeant Major!" and I promptly did just that.

Inside the office the second-in-command and the adjutant were also present. They were both poker faced and after a short pause and looking me up and down at least twice, the CO said, "I've got the general headquarters and the military police on my back so you had better have a bloody good story."

I started at Dover with how I had lost one ATS cook and then the situation on board the ship and how I involved the ship's captain and his number two, the ship's medical officer and the chief petty officer. I told him that as the report had been unfavourable, I had no option but to place the two offenders in confinement with the blessing of the ship's captain.

"That, sir, is how I lost three members of the ATS."

The CO looked around at the other two officers and then back to me. After a short pause he said, "Sergeant Major, I think you did very well and I would like to say thank you, you have got them all off my back. But if called, you will have to give evidence at the court marshal next week on the conduct of these two NCOs. Now, Sergeant Major, I realise you have only just this very moment arrived back on duty with the regiment and I would like to talk to you on a more pleasant subject. In your absence the RSM has left for England to report to Sandhurst Officer Training School in Surrey. We, that is the second-in-command and the adjutant, have talked it over and would like to offer you the post of regimental sergeant major. How do you feel about taking the post?"

I was lost for words but managed to reply, "I would be very honoured and very proud to accept your kind offer, sir."

"That's settled, then. Keep your eye on part-one orders and all three officers."

Now with smiling faces, they warmly offered their congratulations and shook my hand.

I had a quiet night in my rooms, or I should say tent, and went to bed early. I just lay there thinking about my promotion and Rhoda. Just thinking about her and my body was already telling me I was missing her.

In the morning, after showering and shaving, I took a walk around the camp noting any changes that had taken place in the last five months and paid a visit to the other five company sergeant majors, just to say hello and find out if there was any bad feeling about my coming back. I also made mental notes which might come in handy later on.

A midday meal in the sergeants' mess and a visit to the tailors in the afternoon to make the adjustments to my uniforms and at 1600 hrs I walked into the sergeants' mess again, only to be told by a very sleepy orderly that they were not open yet.

"That's all right, I'm just going to sit here for a bit."

That seemed to unsettle him, nevertheless, he came over about 20 minutes later and said, "Sorry to trouble you, sir, but would you like to read today's part-one orders? And congratulations, sir!"

So my promotion had been published. Now everyone would know and I could move into my new quarters.

That evening in the mess I could easily have got inebriated with everyone wanting to buy me drinks. It was then that the lovely voice of Rhoda saved me by saying, "Having a party, Sergeant Major, and not inviting me?"

Rhoda, you have made my day the best day of my life. Come and sit with me and tell me what you have been up to!"

We found a table and everyone could see we needed to be on our own and very politely moved away and showed respect for the new sergeants' mess president and of course, the new regimental sergeant major.

That night I slept very well and first thing in the morning, with my new badge of rank burning a hole on my arm, I started my first morning's walk as RSM. It felt great and I reported to the CO, who once again shook my hand and said, "Let me know if there is anything you need and as from now just report daily to the orderly room for orders."

I then made my way to the mess for breakfast and made arrangements for a table in the centre of the mess alongside a window which overlooked most of the camp to be set aside for my use.

Things had been going very well over the past six months. I had managed to stop tongues wagging by showing I was capable of fulfilling all my duties on the parade ground, in the office and in the field, with the distribution of supplies to the regiment. The icing on the cake was that I was able to see Rhoda most days. She had been promoted to sergeant major and was now in charge of all the catering for the regiment and all the nearby units such as Signals, RASC and REME.

We had become very attached to each other so I had decided to ask her to marry me, only this time my luck and timing had run out; she said she would love to marry me but had been told earlier that day that she had been recommended for officer training and would be leaving in two weeks' time for Sandhurst in Surrey. But all was not lost as I too had good news for her; the regiment, having completed its tour, would be returning to England in six months, so we had a small celebration and set a date for the wedding for July the following year.

Those next six months soon passed. A and B, along with HQ Company, had already arrived back in England. The new incoming regiment's advance party of Royal Marines had arrived and the handover took place. Due to the local unrest we could not use the railway station in Suez for our departure so we had to leave our home for the past three years early in the morning for the two-hour drive to Ismailia. The transport was provided once again by 30th Company Royal Army Service Core, with an escort provided by a fully armed detachment from the Royal

Marines. On our train ride to Port Said and the boat ride home to England, this time no one was lost.

Three weeks to the day and we docked at Dover and waiting for us along the quayside was the regimental band with the regimental colours flying in the wind. It was a day to be proud of and there standing with the wives and children was Rhoda looking more beautiful than ever.

It did not take long for the regiment once, everyone had returned from leave, to start re-equipping and training again and I had also asked for the CO's permission to get married. He congratulated me and said it was about time.

July was not far away and Rhoda and I were busy one weekend in my quarters making guest list seating plans when a knock on the door made us both look up. Standing there was the captain quartermaster.

He said, "I have some news for you both. With the commanding officer's blessing, I'm to inform you that the regiment would be very pleased to make all the arrangements regarding the hall and catering and the use of the barracks' chapel, and the MTO has said he will arrange for transport to and from any pick-up points. And by the way, I have set aside one of the officer's quarters for you to look over.

The wedding day arrived and everything went like clockwork. As we walked out of the chapel, the sergeants' mess guard of honour, made up of every member of the mess, was just perfect. Both Rhoda's and my parents were beaming with pride and all said it was a most perfect wedding.

Cloud Nine

It's 2.00 pm and I've just finished work at the local general hospital. The rain was bucketing down and the high winds were making things very unpleasant. I had about five miles to go and I was not looking forward to the task of pedalling home in this weather.

With my head down I was doing very well. I had about two more miles to go and it was then that I nearly ran into a body sticking out of the bonnet of a very old Ford Escort. I stopped and asked if I could be of some help.

The body straightened out, revealing a very good-looking young man of about 25 years old, 6ft tall and very well built.

He said, "Why don't you do what I'm going to do, sit in The car and wait for it to stop raining?"

I did not think but just got into the car saying to myself, why am I doing this? But nevertheless, I got in and said thank you.

He smiled and said it was his pleasure. He had a lovely smile and I began to relax. We both started to talk at the same time and he said "Ladies first" so I told him that my name was Fay and I was a nursing sister and had just completed my shift and was on my way home in Woodingdean.

He went on to say his name was Dave and he had been on a shoot at the local film studios and was on his way to

Rottingdean to visit his parents but that once more Maybe had shown her temperamental ways and stopped. He must have seen my puzzled look and told me that Maybe was the name he had given his car because it had a mind of its own – maybe it would start or maybe it would not. It was very old but it was his first car which his parents, who lived in Rottingdean had given him and so he was very reluctant to part with it for that reason.

The rain was still pouring down and the conversation went from one subject to the next and I found that I did not want it to stop raining or for the chatting to stop. I have no idea how long we sat there but we both seemed to be enjoying each other's company and kept on talking, even though we both realised that the rain had stopped.

Dave said, "Come on, if Maybe agrees, I'll take you home."

So with a little help from me, we put my bike on the roof of Maybe and with me holding one wheel and Dave holding the other we both waited for Maybe's reaction to Dave turning the ignition key. She must have had a change of heart and burst into life.

Dave said, "She must like you," and we set off, arriving at my home without any mishaps.

Dad must have been watching for me, as usual, and he came running out calling, "What's up? Have you had an accident? Are you hurt?"

Dad had been a police inspector before retirement and had been that much more protective towards me since Mum had been killed in a hit and run incident.

"It's all right, Dad! I met Dave, who very kindly gave me a lift home."

Out of the rain, Dave said, "Good afternoon, sir," and looking over towards me said "I'll be in touch."

As he said those few words I could feel a warm sensation passing through my body and I could feel myself blushing so I grabbed my bike and rushed indoors. Whatever must he think of me? Poor Dave.

It had been six months now since that rainy day and I was ironing my uniform ready for the next day's shift when the doorbell rang.

I could hear Dad saying, "Just a minute, young man, I'll call her." Dad appeared with a great big grin and saying, "Fay, you have a young man called Dave asking to see you." That warm feeling came back when Dad said "Dave".

I showed Dave into the living room and we both sat on the settee. I could feel myself starting to blush so I quickly asked him if he would like a cup of tea or something just to give me a chance to stop thinking about him. He looked very tanned and explained that he had been deep into the South African jungle filming animals for the BBC and did not get a chance to mail me and that his mobile had gone missing at London Airport and would I please forgive him.

It was Dave, and that warm sensation on the back of my neck was telling me something. I said he was forgiven and it was very nice to see him again. It appeared that Dave had built himself a very good reputation while working for the BBC as a specialist cameraman, both in the studio and in the wild, and he had been asked if he would consider taking on doing the portraits of some of the leading stars. He did not need to be asked a second time and had set up a studio in Rottingdean overlooking the sea and cliffs. It would be nice to be able see him more often. The studio had certainly been a great success and lot of local dignitaries and his many friends had made enquiries for sittings. So much so that he had started to work for the BBC only on a part-time basis.

It was lovely to see Dave again and he asked if I would like to go out one evening for a meal and maybe a show. How I stopped myself from shouting out "Yes, yes, I'd Love to!" I don't know. I put it down to my nurse's training and I politely said "I would love to."

Our first evening out went off very well, the show was great and the meal was first class and I now had that feeling of being at ease in Dave's company and hoped he felt the same. We were in contact every day now that Dave worked in Rottingdean and it was so great to hear his voice when he rings. I still get that warm feeling but I don't tell him that.

It's now been four months since our evening out and we three – Dave, Maybe and me – were out in the countryside enjoying the warm sunny day with a small picnic, just lazing on the grass when Dave said, "How about a holiday together somewhere nice and warm?"

This is the first time Dave had shown his feelings towards me and I did not answer right away. I was thinking, Mum, this is when I miss you. Am I ready for such a commitment? I knew I was going to say yes, but just the same I waited a bit longer and said, "Yes, that would be a great idea."

He rolled over and kissed me. We packed up the hamper and blanket and let Maybe take us towards home but somehow we found ourselves walking along the promenade in Brighton holding hands. Dave was chattering away but I did not hear a thing, I was so happy and drifting along on cloud nine. I knew now that I was madly in love with Dave.

Then Dave just stopped walking, put his arms around me and kissed me. I responded most willingly, much to the pleasure of others passing by. I was back on cloud nine and the back of my neck was on fire!

We arrived back at my home and Dad must have been looking out of the window because the door opened before I could get my key out. He had a great smile on his face and called out, "I'll have to get you a key cut, Dave me boy."

I gave Dad a very cold stare and said, "How could you, Dad? Embarrassing Dave like that!"

Dave was just as bad because he replied, "That's a good idea of yours, sir. I would love a key," and with that we all had a good laugh.

I helped Dave out at the studio when I could, acting as secretary, or as it's known "general dogsbody", but I love it and get to see him more often.

It was a Saturday and Dave was closing up and putting his equipment in Maybe when he called out, "Phone your dad and tell him we will pick him up in 20 minutes and all of us are going out for a pub lunch. I've got some good news to tell you both!"

Dad was waiting and we all set off with Maybe's consent. We arrived at The Cock at Ringmer, a very nice place and the food was excellent. We were having after-dinner drinks when Dave just burst out saying, "I've just got to tell my good news. I cannot keep it to myself any longer. I've landed a very good contract with a big drinks company to do all their advertising and they are making me a director and the salary is fantastic. So now that my future is safe," Dave said looking at Dad and then at me, "Fay Collins, with your father's consent, will you please marry me?"

I was stunned as Dave had gone down on one knee and was holding up a beautiful ring. The restaurant being full at the time had gone very quiet but Dad took over the floor by saying, "It would give me the greatest of pleasure to have you as a son," and then everyone was looking at me.

That warm feeling flooded back but this time it had travelled all over. I waited a bit and the restaurant went very quiet again, but then I said, "Yes! I would love to marry you."

The restaurant went wild and everyone was congratulating us. The pub landlord presented us with Champagne and said the meal was on the house.

Dad said, "Things are starting well and let's pray it's a good omen."

We were very lucky and managed to get an early booking for the wedding and we married on 21st July 2006. Dad had pulled all the stops out and gave us a wonderful wedding day.

We both had work commitments so we decided to have Our honeymoon touring in England in the company of Maybe, who had been behaving herself and did not let us down. It must have been all the attention she was getting because she was getting on a bit, but you could see she was getting well looked after.

Time has been good to us and we have moved into our new house in Rottingdean. Dave's work has been very fruitful, what with the studio, the BBC and ITV and with Channel Four showing interest. We have been very fortunate; we now have a dog named Buster and in eight months our family will be a grand total of five, that is Dave, Buster, Maybe, baby and me. With that news, Dave joined me on cloud nine.

Cynthia

Having just returned from making the three o'clock rounds visiting the sentries at our camp just outside Suez in Egypt, the last thing I wanted was to see that our homemade signal bell for the main gate was jumping around like mad. So making a fast response and calling two men to accompany me, on our arrival at the gate we were greeted by a very anxious man who pointed out that the same lorry kept passing.

He said, "I'm sure they are up to no good."

The lorry had turned round and was coming back and they were driving on the wrong side of the road and slowing down. As it got nearer the camp gate, two men on the back pushed an old 40-gallon oil drum off so that it rolled towards the gate. I knew what that meant and called to everyone to get the hell out of there and started to run, but that's when it went off. The blast sent one soldier about ten feet off the ground and he landed 40 feet away. Another had something hit his leg, which broke it and the sentry was unconscious when they found him. I myself, I'm told, was walking around holding my head with blood running from my ears and nose and complaining about the pain. All four of us had received the full blast, causing a great deal of pain.

I somehow made my report to the officer of the day and then just collapsed into his arms. I came to as he was laying me on one of the beds in guard tent and a medical orderly with needle at the ready was saying, "You're on your way to BMH (British Military Hospital), Sergeant Godfrey."

The next morning a gentle voice was saying, "You can wake up now."

At first I just did not want to open my eyes as the pain was still giving me a great deal of concern, but with that very gentle voice and the soft hand on my forehead, I slowly did just that to find I was looking into the face of an angel dressed all in white.

She said, "Would you please tell me your name, number, rank and your regiment?"

I tried to sit up but that voice said, "Not yet, Sergeant," and gently pushed me back down, at the same time plumping my pillow up and saying, "You are to be transferred to a hospital in England in two days so just be a good chap and rest now. Just confirm that you are Sergeant Danny Godfrey of the Royal Sussex Regiment, thank you," and my angel faded away as did the orderly who had given me another shot to help me rest.

On the morning of the second day they gave me another shot of something and I don't remember much of the journey until I was being loaded onto the hospital plane and taking off. That's when I noticed my angel sitting alongside my stretcher.

We landed at Rome for the night and I asked if I could walk, as I was feeling a great deal better now that the headaches were under control. Angel thought about it and said, "If you are sure," and walked with me to the reception desk saying, "He's to have room 12."

I was shown to a very pleasant room with a massive bed and a good view of Rome. Angel said, "I'll be looking in on you a bit later with your medication so get some rest and don't leave the hotel."

Just before 10.00 that night there was a knock on the door and in walked Angel with a tray which she put on the table. She said "I've come to see you get a good night's rest," and with that she undressed, getting into bed with me. I don't know how I managed to get any sleep that night as my angel was very demanding. It was great and for me a night that will remain with me for a very long time. I must have had some sleep because the knocking on the door had me sitting up and looking for my angel. But standing there was a very nice young nurse, saying, "Breakfast in 30 minutes."

I asked where the nurse was that was with me yesterday.

"She left on an early flight," was the reply.

I never saw my angel again but if they are all like that up there, I hope St Peter will let me in, if I should be lucky enough and make it.

I eventually found myself in the London Military Hospital, which I'm told has a very good ear, nose and throat department, and for the next four days I had a thoroughly and extremely good examination. I was then sent to the regimental barracks in Chichester to await the outcome of the report which was to be sent the regiment's medical officer.

It was a very long month later that I found myself having to report to the MO (medical officer) and was sitting in his office watching him read the report of my London examination, which had finally arrived.

The MO looked up, not saying anything for a very long minute and he then said, "Sorry, Sergeant, it's bad news. Your left ear has a partly pierced eardrum and your right has been greatly impaired and will need a great deal of attention, which means I have to start the proceedings for your discharge." He stood up, shaking my hand and saying that he was very sorry.

Three weeks later and with one very old suitcase and a large pack, which the QM had ignored the fact it had not been handed in, I looked around to say my goodbyes to the friends I had made whilst at Chichester but found no one. So I made a slow walk towards the gates of the barracks only to find the whole company waiting for me there, they had not forgotten. After a lot of handshaking, I walked towards the Chichester Station.

I had not got far to go as my family lived just the other side of Brighton at a small village called Peacehaven. Apparently my grandparents had purchased a plot of land under the Gracie Fields' Home for Heroes Scheme and the family still live there. It was a very warm welcome; my mum had a little cry and my dad said, "Come on, let me show you my shed," another way of showing his emotion.

That evening we all went out for a meal at the local pub and that's when I told them the reason for my being there and all about the discharge.

"But you love the army. What will you do now?" said Mum.

I replied, "Well, at first I thought that I would settle down get a job and maybe get married, but now I have that feeling that I would like to have a look around and go to places I've never seen before."

"That will cost a lot of money," said Dad.

"Well, Dad, you see, I have saved my money and my dabbling in stocks and shares has been very fruitful and I now have a nice little nest-egg. I think I'll go a-wandering."

I took the short cut towards my digs and had to pass the motorcycle garage and there, parked on the forecourt, was this gleaming Honda trike in maroon and white livery. I stopped to admire it and was having a good look when out of the garage came two men, one of which was saying in at very high rate, "That's daylight robbery!"

I was about to walk away when this gentleman said to me and indicating towards the other chap, who I took to be the garage owner, "He must be one of the original 40 thieves. Seven thousand indeed!"

I don't know what made me say it but I did, "Seven thousand five hundred would be my offer."

Now that he had quietened down, he looked at me for a good two minutes before saying, "Do you have 20 minutes?"

Well, having all the time in the world, I said yes and he said, "Hop on the back seat."

With that we had a very short ride and pulled into the drive of a large house. He looked me over once again and then said, "Did you mean what you said back there, seven thousand five hundred?"

It was my turn to take a good look at him and then I said, "Yes, that's my offer."

He walked over, shaking my hand and saying, "Once the money is in my bank it's yours."

With that he put the Honda into his garage and handed me the keys. But I could not help but notice the trailer and two sets of leathers and he could see I had seen them.

He then said, "They come with it."

I was truly taken back as all this must have cost far more than I was paying. I was delighted with my Honda and told my parents about my good fortune.

The very next day the landlady called me to the phone. It was the old gent saying the money was in his bank and that I could collect the bike anytime I liked, so I said two o'clock today.

He replied, "I'll be waiting to show you the workings and I have the log book and paperwork ready for you."

It took well over two hours with the paperwork and my meeting Ian's wife, Jill, and a trip down to the local garage to fill up with Ian sitting in the rear seat saying, "Don't forget you have two wheels at the back," a subtle way of saying you're too near the curb.

That night the Honda was parked in Dad's drive and most of the next day, with Dad in the passenger seat, we went to a camping shop where I purchased a tent, primus stove, pots, pans and the many more things that I would need.

That evening I was dressing up in my leathers when my landlady just walked in and despite Mum's warning, it turned out to be a very pleasant night and Kath, the landlady's name, went away with that smile on her face that said thank you.

The night's activities did not stop me from leaving early the next morning for the start of my seeing the rest of England and by midday the Honda, with its new owner, were in Salisbury taking in the beauty of the cathedral spire. After a pub lunch we were putting a few more miles behind us and it was time to stop for the needs of "Hondo" – that's the name I'd given my lovely Honda as I'm a great fan of John Wayne, the film star. I found a campsite, which had all that we both needed and booked in for three nights. I found a place out of the wind, put the tent up, made my bed and a trip to the sites shop that had my dinner and breakfast taken care of.

It was while in the shop that this very nice-looking young girl of about 25 was booking in for three nights and her tent was later pitched about 50 yards away near a gap in the hedgerow.

That night I had a drink in the local pub and the same good-looking young girl was having a meal. While I was chatting to a local character and finding out about any places of interest that might be worth visiting, that's when she left but my pint was only just half full so just had to finish it before leaving. Cutting across the fields towards the gap in the hedge, her tent was the first thing anyone would see and tonight it was truly lit up and her silhouette was for all to see. It was a great sight.

The next morning, while I was cooking my breakfast, she walked past and said, "That smells good."

"Would you care to join me? I always cook too much," and that's how it all started.

"Have I got time to wash and brush up?" she replied.

"I'll have it ready for you."

We got on very well and she told me her name was Cynthia and that she could not sleep at night as the slightest noise made her sit up. That's when I told her about her nightlight and the show she had put on whilst undressing the night before.

I could see her going very red so I put her at ease by saying there was no one but me around and telling a white lie by saying I did not stay to the end. That's when she told me that she was making her way to Bristol and so telling another white lie, I said, "That's my next destination. Why don't you let me take you?"

After a short pause she said, "I have a business partner there that I want to see and so if you are going to the pub tonight, would it be all right if I told you then?"

I just nodded my head to say that would be fine. "Okay, Cynthia," I said, "I'll see you in the pub and the dinner is on me but you can buy the wine."

To my surprise, I spotted her getting into a taxi all dressed up. She looked great.

That evening over dinner I think the wine help out because she told me everything. She'd had a big bust up with her business partner and just walked out and found herself on a hiking holiday. She carried on by saying, "Would you mind helping with my tent? I would like to pitch it closer to yours."

With tongue in cheek I said, "Why don't you put your bed roll in my tent."

She stopped eating and looked at me, smiling, but at the same time said, "I would like that."

So now we were very quiet eating the rest of the meal and that night Cynthia, for the first time in three days, had a good night's sleep.

The next morning I was up bright and early while Cynthia was still sleeping. Breakfast going well and her tent was already rolled up and the packing of the trailer was well in hand when a sleepy head appeared, saying, "Good morning," and with a blanket wrapped round her she made a dash for the wash house and toilets.

For seven months we visited first the west coast into Scotland and down the east coast and it was while we were resting in a hotel in York one night as usual, that I made a call to my parents, only to be told that Cynthia's old partner had somehow got their number was ringing daily. He was desperate to talk to her and so he gave Mum a number so that she could call him.

That call was made the next morning and it turned out to be the end of our happy trip around England. Cynthia and her partner must have been on the phone for nearly an hour when she said, "I'll be with you as soon as I can make the arrangements." She looked very worried and looked over at me saying, "Can we go for a walk so that we can talk?"

We found a bench along the bank of the River Ouse and Cynthia told me about the bust up that led to her walking out. The phone call was one of despair and her partner had told her that as she had not changed the ownership of the salon, she was still the majority shareholder and the suppliers and the bank were going to sue if the outstanding debts were not met by the end if the month.

I said, "If we go back to the hotel, get some shut-eye and leave early in the morning, we could be back in Bristol by tomorrow night. I'll ring my parents and let them know what's going on. You ring and book us in a hotel and we can have this all sorted in two or three days."

We arrived at the hotel later than was expected due to roadworks and went straight to our room, had a shower and rested.

Over breakfast the next morning, Cynthia asked me to accompany her at all the meetings, the first being with her partner, who in my opinion was a very nasty person who right from the start tried domineering tactics with Cynthia and me, which at once had my hackles up.

Looking at Cynthia, I said, "I understand that you have been here on your own due to a misunderstanding, but I also understand the you are the junior partner in this partnership and your attitude is due to you being left to run things. But even so, you are the junior partner and I think you should listen to what Cynthia has to say before you say something that you may regret."

At that point the company solicitor was shown in and said, "I understand that my services maybe required?"

"Yes," Cynthia said, "I'm about to offer Miss Barrett £10,000 for her shares."

I jumped up, saying, "That's far too much!"

Miss Barrett more or less shouted, "I accept!"

I gave Cynthia a wink and the solicitor said, "I can have the papers ready in an hour."

One hour later, having completed the paperwork, Cynthia was now the sole owner of the company and we were being shown into the bank manager's office, who right away said, "I'm so glad you are back. That woman was intolerable to work with and I was considering withdrawing the bank services. But I would be pleased to continue in your case."

The next stop was the suppliers and once the outstanding account had been settled, things were now back on good terms and everyone was once again very happy.

The next bombshell for me was when Cynthia said, "I would like you to get Hondo and Dog and take me to my home in Cleeve and I will tell you all when we get there."

We turned off the A370 into a narrow lane and 500 yards later a big farmhouse with two large barns and surrounded by lots of land suddenly appeared.

"This is my home and I hope you will consider it yours as from now."

I was thunderstruck and did not say anything for a good five minutes. And then, turning to Cynthia, I said, "Let's have a talk with cards on the table." I started by saying, "I have £800,000 in the bank, some stocks and shares, an army pension and Hondo and Dog."

She smiled, saying, "And now you have me and all I own. Shall we get married?"

We married on 21st July and now have two boys and one girl. Latterly things have been going very well and may they continue to do so.